The Ibis Tapestry

The Ibis Tapestry

MIKE NICOL

VINTAGE INTERNATIONAL

Vintage Books

A Division of Random House, Inc.

New York

FIRST VINTAGE INTERNATIONAL EDITION, APRIL 1999

The Library of Congress has cataloged the Knopf edition as follows:
Nicol, Mike,[date]
The Ibis Tapestry: a novel / by Mike Nicol.— 1st ed.
        p   cm.
ISBN 0-679-45507-8
I. Title.
PR9369.3.N54I25 1998
823—dc21   97-50510
CIP

Vintage ISBN: 0-679-78095-5

Author photograph © Jerry Bauer

www.randomhouse.com/vintage

Manufactured in the United States of America
10 9 8 7 6 5 4 3 2 I

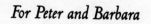

For Peter and Barbara

The author acknowledges a grant received from the Foundation for the Creative Arts during the writing of this book.

PART I

Reconstruction

I

This—once I'd shut out predatory professors, banshees, lawyers, meths-besotted itinerants—is how I imagine it: when Christo Mercer dreams of the death of the four girls for the second time, he is filled with an apprehension bordering on obsession. Looking from his study into the early-morning gardens, where spring has brought back the blossom and the leaves, he sees not the lushness but the girls' bodies lying on the sand. There is no blood. They don't even seem to be wounded, yet still the automatic fire echoes in his head.

I see him mournfully unlock a desk drawer where he keeps—with his passports, cheque book, credit cards, and bank statements—the old exercise book in which he noted all his alarming or recurring dreams. He opens it and writes the date: Thursday, 6 October 1994. Then I see Christo Mercer put down his pen and gaze across the treetops into air that is endless and blue. Blue over the whole continent: a single cloudless sky, an awful anxious blue stretched tightly from horizon to horizon. "Alas, poor fools," he sighs eventually (one of his literary quotes), and, taking up the pen, begins hurriedly to write down what he's dreamt. Even once he's finished his anxiety hasn't lessened. A taste of onions in his mouth won't go away.

As he drives to work, Christo Mercer wonders if the angels are walking as sentinels on the walls of heaven to warn his immortal soul. (Another quote.)

Let me explain: to Christo Mercer dreams were important. They were the diary of his life, a diary he'd first started on the morning of Friday, 21 November 1975. The previous night he'd dreamt of eating lobster: sucking the meat out of the legs, cracking open the tail to reveal the white flesh. When he finished eating, the face that appeared in the plate told him the lobster was poisoned with red tide.

And so the book of dreams was begun. And kept up— secretly—through his seventeen-year marriage to Wilma née Mostert (which occasioned a dream of drowning among yellow fish on the wedding night), the birth of their first daughter, Olive, now aged eleven (a dream of freezing in snow), and then, Emily, now aged seven (falling from a high building). Dreams not only of his death but of the deaths of others. Not necessarily portents or foretellings or prophecies, but often simply visions of horror that caused his chest to constrict with anxiety. As did the dream of the four girls. For one thing it raised an abject memory; for another it presaged a threat; and both caused fear. By the night of Thursday, 6 October, he had become obsessed with the girls to the point of neurosis.

To him they were teenagers wearing jeans and T-shirts with their hair covered in the Muslim way. He pictured them walking out of an old walled town, then being gunned down. He could see this mud town of mosques and casbah, alleys, lanes, wells, date palms, the houses rising against one another cool and shuttered, the stench of camel dung in the streets, a town that could be in Mali, Libya, Chad, or Morocco, anywhere in Saharan Africa. Towns he knew well: whether Malitia, where he had an office, or Djano, where he sometimes stayed with the old warlord Ibn el-Tamaru, or Bilo, Misana, Taghazi, and Murzuk, where he'd met an array of men wanting to buy arms and ammunition. From some of these places he had recurring dreams—of burning, desiccation, garotting—and those places he tried not to revisit. He went by the old adage:

Dream a dream thrice
cockatrice.

Which was the other reason Christo Mercer felt the angels were warning his immortal soul, and made him anxious not to dream of these deaths a third time.

Moreover, it was with the second dream that he realized the town was Djano. As he closed the exercise book and locked it away in the drawer, he considered delaying his trip there. But in the end he decided merely to be cautious. That afternoon he faxed his people in the northern office asking them to tell the customers he would be in Malitia later in the month but unable to journey to outlying towns such as Djano. He was hopeful that Ibn el-Tamaru would consider the journey to see him worthwhile, but about the others, particularly the Englishman, he was less confident. He would not be as accommodating. He would . . .

What?

Christo Mercer went back to wondering about the girls. He gave them names he took from a file of foreign newspaper clippings about the wars in his territory. His territory—his empire—was extensive, covering most of the Sahara. So the girls became Farida, Dirie, Gali, Salma.

When he got home that evening, the evening of Thursday, 6 October 1994, an e-mail message from the Englishman was waiting for him.

Go away, Justine, you bitch. I'm not opening the door. I'm trying to write a serious book, for Christ's sake!

2

Christo Mercer's study overlooked the suburban gardens of Waterkloof, Pretoria. I have stood in that room (Sunday, 1 October 1995) and noted the view: just the sort of detail every writer needs as he begins the process of reimagining a life.

The house itself is a double-storey mock-Tudor with leaded windows. Shortly after he became a director of International Ventures, sometime early in 1986, he bought the house. He was captivated by anything that hinted at old England. He thought of this house—with six bedrooms, three bathrooms, study, two lounges, family room, large kitchen including a breakfast nook, dining room, pantry, and laundry—as his "cottage." When he arrived home at the end of the day and the automatic gates locked behind him across the driveway, then he considered himself safe.

Like so many in the suburbs, Christo Mercer believed he was living in a state of siege. The statistics, I suppose, supported this belief. For instance, in late 1994 a survey reported that every hour of each day some ninety-nine violent crimes were committed, including the rape of three women and the murder of two people.

So it is hardly surprising that as the country became increasingly prone to suburban violence Christo Mercer took precautions. In 1988 he had a high wall fringed with barbed metal spikes built around the perimeter. He had burglar bars fastened to the windows and security grilles bolted onto all the doors, especially the double doors opening from the lounge onto the patio and swimming pool; at the top of the staircase another metal grille secured the bedrooms at night. He had two Alsatians called Chaka and Dingaan. His house was wired to an armed response unit. Locked in a safe in his study were a Magnum .357 pistol, an R1 automatic rifle, an AK-47, and a side-by-side Smith & Wesson shotgun. He was also storing five hundred rounds of ammunition.

To me this speaks of a siege mentality.

Waterkloof is a suburb of large houses set in large grounds—not unlike the Cape Town suburb from which I was evicted three months ago. A suburb of swimming pools and tennis courts. A suburb of lawns, gardeners, beds of rhododendrons. The streets are lined with jacaranda trees, which in September blossom into purple and in October lay this purple on the pavements.

The people of Waterkloof do not walk; they drive. They drive to their offices in the city, they drive to the shopping malls, they drive their children to school. The cars they drive are usually made by Mercedes-Benz or BMW. Christo Mercer drove one of the latter. The people who live in Waterkloof are ambassadors, consuls, military attachés, bankers, corporate executives, senior civil servants. As a director of International Ventures, Christo Mercer was not out of place.

Before the Mercer house was sold in October 1995, the estate agent opened it as a show house for two consecutive Sundays. On those two days it was available as a sort of Christo Mercer museum, so I went there to wander among the Sanderson floral sofas he had sat on when he entertained or read the Sunday papers. I stared at the prints of English racehorses hung in wide gold-leafed frames. I felt the weight of the silver candlesticks placed at the end of the mantelpiece. I couldn't resist smelling the richness of the sherry he kept in crystal decanters on a sideboard. I marvelled at how well stocked his liquor cabinet was.

In the family room I tried out the morris chair he lounged in to watch television or listen to music. There is something peculiar about sitting in a dead man's chair. Like sitting on someone's lap, it's intimate and uncomfortable.

Among Christo Mercer's CDs I noted a propensity for masses and requiems (four different versions of Mozart's Requiem), some jazz (mostly Keith Jarrett), a full collection of Crosby, Stills and Nash, and a curious assortment of musicians from western Africa: Ali Farka Touré, Salif Keita, the sound of Wassoulou, Youssou N'Dour, Ismael Lô.

In the dining room I sat down at the yellow-wood table where he took his meals. (Fortunately, the estate agent was too busy with prospective buyers to supervise my personal tour.)

Upstairs I stood in his daughters' bedrooms (immaculate neat pink rooms); in the main bedroom I wondered on which side of the king-sized bed he had slept. I smelt the pillows for a trace of his scent but detected only fabric softener. I felt the mattress for its spring. I would have ignored the dressing table with its jars of cream and glass ornaments had I not stooped to glance at myself in the mirror and seen instead, stuck in the mirror's frame, a colour photograph of Christo Mercer. This I pulled loose.

What struck me first was the size of his head. Too big, too heavy, too old, it didn't belong to his body. He had jowls. His hair was thin, the dome of his forehead gleamed in the sun. His lips were closed, he didn't smile, his eyes had no light.

"How do you do, Christo Mercer," I said aloud, for a moment forgetting where I was.

He stood on a beach wearing swimming trunks and an unbuttoned shirt. A blue towel was bunched in his right hand, sunglasses dangled from the other. His body was in no worse condition than mine: ordinary, neither fat nor thin, no bones showing, no obvious muscles, a slight swelling at the gut, hairy legs and arms. Only the head didn't match. With a head like that he should've been as thickset as a dictator. At his shoulders the azure of the sky met the cyan of the sea—which seemed to disembody him, to let his head float free.

I pocketed the photograph and continued my exploration. In the wardrobe: a neat line of suits, a collection of ties, white ironed shirts, rows of shoes, fifteen pairs in all.

In the bathroom I found three bottles of men's aftershave: Dolce & Gabbana, Armani, Paco Rabanne. Wilkinson's shaving foam. Prep shaving cream. Razor blades for a Gillette Contour. Safari for Men deodorant. An old black comb with dirt at the start of the teeth and caked in between. I noted that what was missing was a toothbrush, razor, nail clippers, brush: the items he would take on a business trip.

In his study I listed the books: Marlowe, Shakespeare, Kyd, Tourneur, Webster, all the Elizabethans great and small. Nothing else, just the Elizabethans.

On his desk were photographs of his wife and daughters. The background to the pictures didn't locate them anywhere.

I opened the desk drawer—the key was in the lock—and riffled through his bank statements (healthy credit balances), details of his mortgage repayments (the loan almost paid off), credit card slips (mostly for restaurants), bond certificates (numerous), the portfolio of his stock exchange investments (impressive), and a ten-page essay typed on a manual typewriter and dated 1985. But then I heard the estate agent climbing the stairs. I slid the drawer closed and sat at Christo Mercer's desk looking out over the trees and roofs of Waterkloof as he had done almost exactly a year previously.

I imagined him writing down his second dream of the death of the four girls on the morning of Thursday, 6 October 1994. The trees then, as now, would have been full-leafed, fresh with here and there the purple of a late-flowering jacaranda. The brown and the dust of winter were gone. The lawns were green again. The brunfelsia was in mauve-and-white flower; its scent and that of jasmine were the perfume of the night. This time of year Christo Mercer called the "English days."

"It's a fine property, don't you think?" said the agent.

She was one of those women for whom the short thigh-length skirt was fashioned. All my women wear such skirts: it's how they ensnare their men. Spies, mercenaries, arms dealers, drug barons, diamond magnates, and stockbrokers are stricken alike before them, paralyzed, their eyes compelled to slide up those long shapely legs that strut from the tight material where all promise is moulded yet aggressively withheld. Needless to say, my eyes were similarly enraptured.

"Don't you think?" she repeated.

I agreed it was, and left.

On the next Sunday (8 October 1995) I revisited the house to verify a few details.

"Weren't you here last week?" asked the agent, her legs this time sheer in navy tights.

I nodded.

"There's been a few offers. But nothing's signed and sealed yet," she said.

"I'd need my wife to see it before we can commit ourselves," I said.

My wife! That's a joke.

"Do you mind if I look round again?"

"Help yourself." She smiled.

I noticed details I hadn't seen before: the ivory-handled sword leaning against the wall in the second lounge, an old kelim hanging on the staircase wall. But most importantly, in the study a small crucifix on a chain was pinned to the book-shelf above the desk.

3

This on my answering machine (Friday, 17 November 1995):

"Hello, Robert, it is Richard here. You must surely be back from your travels by now. Nobody could possibly stay in Malitia longer than ten days; it sounds a perfectly sordid place. How did things go? Did you find out why your mysterious Christo Mercer was killed? Or should I say did you get to the bottom of the matter?—if you'll excuse the pun. [Jolly *ho-ho* laughter.] Do give me a call so that we can arrange to meet for that elusive drink. I'm curious to hear all your news. Ciao for now!"

"Robert, I know you're back, and when I come knocking at your door I expect you to open it. I also expect you to pick up the receiver and talk to me. Me. Justine. You can't just ignore me. I know you're listening. Come on, pick it up. Robert! Robert, damn you, pick it up! You can't hide behind that machine forever. For God's sake, stop acting like a teenager. You've got obligations, you know. You've got obligations to Matthew and Luke. They're your sons. This is screwing Luke up. You can't just pretend they don't exist. Jesus, Robert, you can be an arsehole. It's no wonder I felt you were driving me out of my mind."

"Good morning, Mr. Poley, this is Ursula, Mr. Melnick's secretary. He wonders if it would be possible to arrange a meeting for three p.m. on the twenty-first. Apparently there are some new matters which have to be discussed before a final divorce settlement can be drawn up. Also he says to let you know he doesn't see this going to court until sometime in January."

"Hullo, dear, it's your mother. If you can, please call round over the weekend. Bye."

With all this to work against, how am I expected to concentrate?

However.

4

The e-mail message from the Englishman to Christo Mercer read: "Christo, whatever you're up to don't renege. Let's just say it wouldn't be in the interests of your livelihood. We'll see you in Malitia."

The message was signed with the initials NS.

5

To reconstruct: that is the researcher's task. To find the life among the few scattered details and piece together some motive for why something happened. Also to *imagine*, to make the leap from a fact to the emotion it elicited. Which is hardly scientific, but what is these days? Stephen Hawking wants a Theory of Everything. Don't we all! But to get from here to Everything will take educated guesswork, which most probably will never become anything more than that. My reconstruction follows the same principle. Start from facts, reality, what is known. When the gaps come, jump—but only if there's something out there to land on. I'm not making anything up. I'm reporting.

So, to begin. I can think of no better moment than that October night when Christo Mercer sat in his study looking out over the dark gardens of Waterkloof. The taste of onions was still in his mouth, raising a memory he thought he'd long forgotten. Or rather, a memory he'd learnt not to remember. One which even now he kept hidden from himself.

On his desk was a flask of coffee; next to it a plastic pill bottle of amphetamines he'd bought at the Avalon Pharmacy in Beatrix Street. He was using both stimulants in a desperate bid to stay awake. To borrow from the immortal bard—although I shouldn't because, as I shall show, Christo Mercer's idée fixe was that other Elizabethan giant, Christopher Marlowe—to sleep would be perchance to dream and that was the last thing my subject wanted.

The first thing my subject wanted—I'm assuming this, of course, but on good authority—was to see if his fax to Malitia had caused any "ripples in the universe," which is the way I would normally phrase such things.

So, pumping with uppers and caffeine, he plugged in his laptop and track-balled his way to his cyberspace postbox, where the foreboding e-mail from NS awaited him. A message of electronic impulses, a virtual message, a troubling reality he could not ignore.

Here I have to jump from fact to imaginative reconstruction. He downloaded the message to his hard drive and stored it in a file named, somewhat amusingly and therefore, in Christo Mercer's case, somewhat surprisingly, "e-pisodes." I don't know what reaction he had to the warning from NS. If he got up and stared out into the darkness feeling it contained all danger and all evil. If the fascination of the words made him read them again and again and again until they accelerated his heart rate to alarming levels. If he checked his guns, if he went round the house locking all the doors and windows, if he made any telephone calls. I just don't know.

Except. Except that he must have got up from his desk and gone to his bookshelf and selected a book—haphazardly? for distraction? on purpose? because he remembered something?—and become preoccupied with it. He entered its world. Nothing strange about this, since people do it all the time; it's called reading, or escapism, or swapping realities. The thing about Christo Mercer is that he went one step further: he wanted his own fantasy, so he started writing it.

How do I know?

I know this because sometime on that Thursday night he opened a file in his word processor called "virgins.txt." He then typed a large segment from this book he'd selected, followed by, one below the other, the four names he'd found by scanning through the newspaper clippings. He ignored the real lives of Farida, Dirie, Gali, Salma. Instead he fictionalized them.

Thus (and I summarize):

To him, Farida was the most beautiful of them all. Her skin was as glossy as molasses, unblemished. She had almond eyes, a delicate nose, high cheekbones, soft velvet lips. Her father was a musician and her mother was dead. Her father was famous and had played in Paris, Berlin, London, New York, Tokyo. They called him Le Popstar. From his travels he'd brought her back sunglasses, transistor radios, the just-released records of the dreadlocked Bob Marley, jeans, a poster of Muammar Qaddafi, another of Haile Selassie, French copies of *Vogue*. She could read and write French. She hadn't been circumcised. She wanted to be a model. She was the best dressed of the four as they walked towards the gunmen on a day at the end of the nineteen-sixties.

She hated living in Djano. She wanted to live in New York. She'd never been out of Djano but she could imagine New York. She wanted to live where there was rain and snow and the lakes froze. But more than that she wanted electricity. And she wanted the colours green, black, grey. She couldn't stand the browns and ochres of Djano. It was a town of dry mud. To her it was a place of the crippled and the malformed and the crazy with drool on their chins. It was a town of camels and donkeys. She wanted a city of cars. She wanted a city of pavements where people were dressed in the fashions of *Vogue* or *Elle* or *Paris Match*. She wanted water and muted light and an air the colour of tarnished silver. She wanted a sun that was distant: not a heat but a glow that would touch her skin gently. She wanted a great city built of concrete and glass. She wanted a river, a harbour, highways. She wanted a city of light. A city that dimmed the stars. She wanted New York.

Farida was fourteen years old.

Gali was fifteen. She was the exact opposite of Farida. Not that she was ugly, only that her face was flatter and her skin sallow. She probably ate too much fat. She wasn't wearing jeans. She wore a brownish dress from which the colour had long been washed. She was barefoot. She came from a poor family. She was tagging behind the other three girls as they walked out of the town.

Her parents were both alive, although her father was little better than a living dead man who hadn't spoken a word or cured a hide since the death of his mother. Once people had called him the finest tanner between Djano and Timbuktu, and his racks had always been full of salted pelts. But now her mother did the tanning while he sat on a stool in the yard, unmoving even when flies crawled on his face.

Gali, being the eldest, helped her mother with the skins. She salted and limed and worked in fat to soften the hair on the pelts. Or she checked on her father, to make sure he hadn't died, and fed him the food he wouldn't eat himself.

Yet Gali sang as she worked. She sang the songs her mother sang about love and death and good times and bad times and the birth of fat babies, but the words meant nothing to her. Gali didn't expect anything of life. She couldn't imagine another way of being. She didn't know her hands were hard and cracked. She didn't know what it meant to read and write. At five she had been raped by an uncle; at nine she'd been circumcised. She didn't know that her mother was planning to sell her to a man as old as her father. As she walked towards the gunmen she was the one least terrified.

Dirie?

Dirie was circumcised but had not been raped. As the four of them walked across the sand she was just slightly behind Farida, who, predictably, was in front. Dirie wore plastic thongs on her feet, her jeans were patched, her T-shirt had a Ban the Bomb symbol on the front (it had been given to her in exchange for a bagful of dates by a young Swiss motorbiker passing through some months before). Under her scarf Dirie had hair that would spill about her shoulders like silk when she let it loose; it was black, it was rich, it could be admired only in the mirrors of her room. When Dirie smiled she showed teeth so white they were almost translucent.

Dirie's father worked on distant oil wells and was at Djano for only a month each year. Her mother was a typist for the Gouverneur. She'd visited Marseilles and Paris when she was Dirie's age. Dirie had photographs of her standing at the Eiffel Tower. In one of them she was with Dirie's grandfather, who had once been the *sous préfet* at Djano. All she could remember of him was the smell of aniseed. She couldn't remember him dying.

At the age of eight Dirie went to M. Vincent's school. She learnt to read and write in French. She began to wonder at the world that lay beyond the sand. She listened to Farida's Bob Marley records. She coveted the poster of Muammar Qaddafi. She had her own pair of sunglasses, her own transistor radio. She read Farida's magazines. She'd written letters to Warren Beatty and Sasha Distel. She wanted to live in Paris. But she didn't want to be a model. She wanted to be the newly married Jackie Onassis and walk the quai along the Seine.

Dirie was fourteen years old.

Salma, the last and the youngest, was thirteen. She was the one Christo Mercer saw most clearly. He could see the fineness of her lashes when she closed her eyes. Then, without those sad Kalamata eyes to distract him, he could picture the sharp lift of her cheeks, the oval line of her jaw, the lips slightly parted and the hint of teeth behind them. He imagined the faint warmth of breath coming from her nostrils. He gave her the fine nose of an Arabian princess.

Salma was a refugee. She hadn't been born in Djano. She'd been there only three years when she was chosen to face the gunmen. Her mother and father had gone to Djano because they'd thought it was a place so out of the way that they'd be safe there. They wanted a town that knew nothing of bloodletting, of corpses in the street, of the hourly terror of dying. A town for their daughter. They wanted this because they'd been forced to flee from so many places carrying what they could: the elderly, the children, food. Too often they'd looked back at villages that had become pillars of flame, or they'd walked through fields of burnt crops, the air still black and falling with ash. Too often they'd had to bury their kin along the road, as they'd had to bury Salma's younger sister and brother. Too often they'd been raped and beaten. And so for them Djano was a sanctuary beyond the reach of warring men. Protected by the desert, it was untouchable.

Salma's father was a candlemaker, a good occupation in a town where the generator powered only the fans and the lights in the Gouverneur's office and home. Her mother grew herbs in the garden beside the well. Salma helped them both. When M. Vincent tried to persuade them to let Salma attend his school, they argued that they needed her help. According to custom Salma had been circumcised when she was ten years old; although the wound had turned septic, her mother's herbs had kept her alive. Once she reached the age of fifteen, her parents expected to sell her to a marriageable man. For such a beauty they anticipated a good price.

Salma knew about Bob Marley. She knew about transistor radios. Djano was not so big a town that she could fail to know of these things. Like most of the other young people in Djano—even Gali—she would rush to stand outside Farida's house whenever Le Popstar was practicing with his band. But Salma didn't know about *Vogue* or *Elle* or *Paris Match*. She didn't know about New York or Jackie Onassis. She couldn't imagine electricity. She could imagine a husband and children. She could imagine her life as the Qur'an said it would be.

On the morning Salma walked out of the town gates with Farida and Dirie and Gali she was dressed in old jeans and a T-shirt supplied by USAID. She wore leather sandals; her head scarf was pale blue and embroidered. She looked back once at the people gathered on the wall and clustered at the gate, and moments after that the shooting started.

And then Christo Mercer typed the name of the town: Djano.

Some time early in the morning (at least in my reconstruction) and well before dawn, his wife, Wilma, appeared in the study.

"Kom nou, Christo," she said, "you can't work all night."

He looked up from the screen. A little icon with a smile on its face was leaping at random about the dark rectangle. He realized he hadn't typed anything for some time.

"I won't be long," he said.

"You don't have to do this," she said.

Christo Mercer touched the space bar, and the screen lit up. He saw the last word he'd typed was Djano.

"I do," he said.

"You'll make yourself ill. No one's asking you to do that."

"Don't worry, Wilma," he said. "I won't be long."

Djano. A town founded on salt. For five hundred years black

slaves had mined its deposits, salt caravans had passed through its jurisdiction, rich men had lived within its walls. In September 1894, after a two-week battle that left hundreds dead, the French had marched through its gates and had marched out again only in April 1968, leaving a Gouverneur to look after their interests during the transition to self-rule. Less than two years later the warlord Ibn el-Tamaru made the town his citadel and the Gouverneur was executed by firing squad.

Djano was one of the towns Christo Mercer had visited on his first trip in 1986. He'd gone there to sell Ibn el-Tamaru an assortment of light weaponry. The journey from Malitia had taken three days. He could remember watching the town shimmering on the desert flats as he was driven towards it.

At a distance Djano seemed to float above the plain; as they got closer it settled and he could make out the houses piled and terraced on a hill. The towers of a mosque rose among them. The town was ringed by an old mud wall that in places had collapsed and crumbled away. Ibis stalked along the wall like sentinels. They drove through the gates into a maze of arches and tunnels and balconies and narrow lanes and doorways opening onto dim interiors. People called out to them, children ran behind the Jeep. They went along a shadowed street into a souk loud with trade. Christo Mercer waited in the Jeep with his translator while the driver sought out their customer, the warlord. About him smiling faces dipped and nodded, offering strange foods and wanting to buy Eveready batteries, ballpoint pens, denim clothing.

That evening Christo Mercer stayed in the house of Ibn el-Tamaru. He was introduced to the warlord's wife, Sarra, and to a crippled young woman, Salma, who leant on a stick and showed some pain in her face as she walked.

"Is she your daughter?" he asked when the women were gone.

"No," said the warlord. "That is what she has become."

And then he said, "I am a simple man, Mr. Mercer. Allah is my God and I am his wrath. The Qur'an is his word and although I cannot read it, I obey it. When I was young Allah spoke to me, and I have listened to him ever since. Those who have heard the voice of Allah must obey. Should Allah decide to praise or punish there is no other course but acceptance."

He explained that as a boy he'd herded goats. That one day he found another goatherd at his well, a boy his age. The two goatherds eyed each other and the goats milled about, rampant and butting in their want to get water.

This well was among rocks: a spring that rose in a pool and shaded always by the huge pink stones surrounding it. The young Ibn el-Tamaru considered this well to be exclusively his own. No tracks except his led to it, and no other goatherds brought their flocks to browse these saltbush flats. Whether it was ancient lore or merely the well's distance from their camps and villages that kept others away he didn't know. He went there for the solitude. In this place he could stand and know that in the circle of his vision no other person moved. Until this day.

When the clatter of goats brought the realization that his sanctuary, his kingdom, had been violated, he stood abject. He was even going to walk away. Then slowly he went towards the well.

"Do you see how Allah works?" said Ibn el-Tamaru. "He presents the choice and you are left to chose."

So they stood looking at each other, the two youths. The goats belonging to the other boy were trying to climb out of the rock enclosure, while the young Ibn el-Tamaru's flock pressed towards the water. Eventually the turmoil ceased.

"I told him he was not to use this well again. I said I would chase him away if I found him there. But he didn't listen to me. When I next caught him there we fought with sticks. Another time we fought with our whips. Finally we used knives. It was inevitable what was going to happen. One of us had to die. As you can see he was that one. The goatherd knew I was stronger; I had beaten him many times. He knew he would die yet he couldn't resist. And since then it has been the same with others who have challenged me.

"Do you know that I am called the Prince of Destruction? But that is by people who fail to see the truth. They look at the waste of wars but not at what issues from them. They do not see the rebirth, the regeneration, the chance to re-create. I have given opportunity. I have allowed people to dream again of what they would become. They could reimagine themselves. This is what I have given. And so it would be better if they named me the Prince of Resurrection, do you not agree?

"Let me tell you, Mr. Mercer, in this world it is the weak who need the strong. When the weak grow fat and lazy and stink of rot then they need the ritual of cleansing. That is how it was here at Djano before I came. The Gouverneur was a thief. He took bribes; he stole taxes. He wanted me to stop the decay of his rule. I did what he wanted. It is only natural. Historians will tell you this. Philosophers will tell you this. Cities are founded on the ruins of razed cities. Beneath are always ruins and bones. Our mortar is blood. It is how we build. By our pattern the weak sacrifice themselves to the strong. They want it that way; and we both understand there is no alternative. This is why there are people like you and me, Mr. Mercer."

That night Christo Mercer dreamt he was walking down a cobbled road, the houses on either side in such darkness that he couldn't see them. It started to rain. Beneath his feet the cobbles sprouted long green shoots until he was walking through a forest and could no longer see the road or where it led. When he woke he realized the cobbles had been not stones but onions.

Ibn el-Tamaru proved to be a good contact. Over the years

Christo Mercer sold more rifles, land mines, and mortars to the warlord of Djano than to anyone else in his territory.

"These are not for me," the warlord would tell him solemnly. "I have no use for such things anymore. Maybe one day in the future, perhaps. A man can never tell what Allah plans. But not now."

Yet Ibn el-Tamaru was known wherever trouble stirred. He took Christo Mercer to places so remote and empty there seemed to be no reason why anyone should fight over wastes this hopelessly forlorn. But there were those who did and had done so for hundreds of years. He took him to places where the killing was unlike anything Christo Mercer had ever seen. He showed him Christian churches filled with corpses. He showed him burnt mosques where charred human bones lay stacked and strewn. Neither of them ever commented on these things.

Outside the old town of Fort Jado he showed Christo Mercer the wreckage of a Messerschmitt; its wings had fallen upon the sand and sand was piled against its fuselage. Like all that died in the desert this was a skeleton: metal bent and skinned with rust, disintegrating. Ibn el-Tamaru walked round it as if admiring a monument.

"You know what this is," he said. "It is from the Germans. It came to this village where there was no war, where the people did not even know there was a war, and it started shooting. I don't know how many were killed. But Allah is just. Because this is where the German died. Here in his plane. This is where he crashed. And do not ask why. We cannot know the mind of God."

6

We cannot know the mind of God. That much is true. It's also true that we can't even know the mind of another man—or woman. My own wife's a goddamned mystery! For God's sake! What does the woman think she's doing?

I don't know. I just don't know. Whatever, whatever, whatever.

To get back to Christo Mercer. To the mind of Christo Mercer. The truth is, I don't know what was going on in his mind. I can only recount, put disparate facts together, reinvent, describe, collect evidence, reimagine, present. And what I have to present next is another e-mail.

This was downloaded onto his hard drive at 3:10 a.m. on Friday, 7 October 1994:

We need words of reassurance, Christo. We need to be placated. We need to be soothed. We need to be told that you still love us. When plans change we get insecure, Christo. We don't know what the change means. We think maybe you're jilting us. Give us hope, Christo. Tell us nothing has changed. Just don't disappoint us; we wouldn't want any harm to come to you. NS

If Christo Mercer responded to this, there is no record of it. However, I'm intrigued that at that desperate hour of the morning he thought to check for e-mail. Did he expect NS would not let him off with one cryptic advisory? I must conclude he did.

Does this indicate insecurity, vulnerability, foreboding, or simple fear? I think it does. All of these things. Clearly NS was a man who unsettled Christo Mercer.

But if this is more educated guesswork, I can also offer facts which, in themselves, say something about what was going on in his mind. For instance, "virgins.txt" concerns some scenes from Christopher Marlowe's play *Tamburlaine the Great*, where four virgins are summarily executed.

Let me recount: the mighty warlord Tamburlaine is laying siege to Damascus. His army is camped about the walls of the city; his men have grown bored and irritable from inactivity and the flies. Not a single blow has been struck, not a wound opened. Tamburlaine himself is growing ever more impatient with the governor's wheedling and pleading and stalling as they haggle over the terms of a surrender settlement. He dislikes the governor. He considers him cowardly and cunning. He doesn't trust him. His impatience is verging on anger. He's given the governor every chance of a peaceful solution, but still the man dallies.

The reason for the governor's expediency is the slim hope that the Soldan of Egypt might arrive in time to save the city and decimate the marauding forces. Despite Tamburlaine's reputation for violence, the governor is prepared to risk lives in this mad gamble. And so the game is played out until the morning the city wakes to find the invading army's tents adorned with coal-black colours, and the warmonger himself dressed all in black.

Act V, scene i: the governor and the four virgins, holding branches of laurel, stand at the gates of the city looking out at the black tents.

The governor says to the virgins, You're our only hope. If we sued for peace now he'd sack the city nonetheless. I fear the custom proper to his sword. So let us place your harmless lives in his hands and hope this will melt his fury.

The first virgin (could she be reconstructed as Christo Mercer's Farida?) replies that if only the governor had listened to the entreaties of the women of Damascus, then perhaps they wouldn't now be facing this death warrant.

The governor brushes her off. Lovely virgins, think of your city. I couldn't allow us to be overrun while there was a chance of rescue. But now your lives, as much as ours, are at stake and we have either to endure the malice of our stars and the wrath of Tamburlaine or hope your cheerful looks will bring us pardon.

Farewell, sweet virgins, on whose safe return
Depends our city, liberty, and lives!

> *Exeunt [all except the Virgins]. Enter Tamburlaine dressed in black and very melancholy, and some of his lieutenants*

To the virgins Tamburlaine says, Why didn't they send you out earlier? Can't they see it's too late for submissions? They know my custom. And now you'll be the first to feel the sworn destruction of Damascus.

Pity our plights! O, pity poor Damascus, pleads the first virgin. Pity the old people and the babies, pity everyone living in this wretched town.

Do you see this sword? says Tamburlaine. What do you see at the point?

Nothing but fear and fatal steel, my lord, answers the first virgin.

Then your minds are too fearful to think straight, says Tamburlaine. For there sits Death. Just as his fleshless body also feeds from the points of my horsemen's spears.

Techelles, he calls to the group of lieutenants, go and order some of my horsemen

To charge these dames, and show my servant, Death,
Sitting in scarlet on their armed spears.

VIRGINS: O, pity us!
TAMBURLAINE: Away with them, I say, and show them Death!

I speculate: no, Christo Mercer says to himself, no. It doesn't happen like that.

But he knows it does. He's seen it; he's done it.

And, remember, twice he's dreamt of the deaths of the four girls as they walked out of the town of Djano to face the AKs.

7

All of which, firstly, briefly, by way of corroborative digression, brings me to the Unabomber.

And, secondly, verbosely, in the interests of explication, brings me to Professor Richard Khafulo. Who is a man given to poetic metaphors. "Literature exposes the buried bones of lived experience." Or, "One must never underestimate the archaeological quality of some prized works" (both quotes, 13 September 1995).

Whatever.

From the *Washington Post*'s Internet site—accessed at the I-Café down the road where I go to "surf" the international press—comes this (edited) revelation:

"In Joseph Conrad's novel *The Secret Agent*, a brilliant but mad professor abandons academia in disgust for the isolation of a tiny room, his 'hermitage.' There, clad in ragged, soiled clothes, he fashions a bomb used in an attempt to destroy an observatory derisively referred to as 'that idol of science.'

"Federal authorities believe Theodore J. Kaczynski, the former mathematics professor who loved Conrad's works well enough to read them repeatedly, may have fashioned his life upon the 1907 novel. Even before identifying Kaczynski as a suspect in the Unabomber case, FBI agents noted the parallels between Conrad's theme of science as a false icon and the Unabomber's targeting of scientists and technological experts and his condemnation of technology in letters to news organizations [and his long manifesto published in the *New York Times* and the *Washington Post* in September 1995].

"Investigators sent *The Secret Agent* and other Conrad works to scholars last summer, hoping for insights into the mind of a killer who eluded them for eighteen years.

"With Kaczynski's arrest the parallels fall neatly into place. Kaczynski, a brilliant man who had been psychotically troubled most of his life, fled academia for a hermit's existence in a Montana shanty, where, grossly unkempt, he lived for a time off turnips he grew behind his cabin. One of the anarchists in the novel lived on a diet of raw carrots.

"Federal agents say they believe that Kaczynski used Conrad or Konrad as an alias on at least three occasions while staying at a hotel in Sacramento where he allegedly went to mail bombs. By coincidence, Conrad's birth name is given either as Teodore Jozef Konrad Korzeniowski or Jozef Teodore. Kaczynski's full name is Theodore John Kaczynski.

"Kaczynski's alleged use of the initials 'FC' on a number of bombs and in letters to news organizations is yet another similarity. The Unabomber's letters said the initials stood for 'Freedom Club.' In *The Secret Agent,* anarchists use the initials 'FP' or 'Future of the Proletariat' in their leaflets.

"Kaczynski, who is charged with killing two people and injuring six others in a total of seven bombings, grew up with Conrad's complete works in his family's suburban Chicago home. During twenty-six years in the Montana wilderness, he pored over Conrad's writings. In a 1984 letter to his family he said he was reading Conrad's novels for 'about the dozenth time.' Characters in *The Secret Agent* may provide a rare glimpse into Kaczynski's mind—and his view of himself."

I cite his case merely because it throws a light on literary obsessions. So, to continue: Christo Mercer, according to his

sister, memorized whole speeches from Elizabethan plays. At
night he would spend long hours reading aloud into his tape
recorder; in the mornings, on his way to work, he played the
cassettes over the car stereo.

Call for the robin red breast and the wren,
Since o'er shady groves they hover,
And with leaves and flow'rs do cover
The friendless bodies of unburied men.
Call unto his funeral dole
The ant, the field-mouse, and the mole
To rear him hillocks, that shall keep him warm
And (when gay tombs are robb'd) sustain no harm,
But keep the wolf far thence: that's foe to men,
For with his nails he'll dig them up again.

He would recite along with his recorded voice, and other com-
muters locked in the slow-moving traffic would stare at this
balding, long-faced man in his bright tie and white shirt, his
face animated with words, and smile.

Christo Mercer had read some two hundred fifty Elizabethan
plays; but Marlowe, above all, was the one who fascinated him.

As I've mentioned, in the drawer of his desk was an unpub-
lished monograph entitled "The Nature of Political Power in
Marlowe's *Tamburlaine the Great.*" Stapled to it was a letter from
the editor of the academic journal *English in Africa,* making sug-
gestions and comments and offering to reconsider the paper
once it had been reworked. But Christo Mercer never got round
to rewriting the essay. Why not? Pressure of work! Loss of
interest! Loss of conviction! Who knows? (There are hundreds
of useful excuses.)

In those days (1985) he believed in the State of Emergency.

Then he was convinced of the "total onslaught." He had noted parallels between Tamburlaine's relentless aggression and the attitudes of generals like Magnus Malan. And it was this spirit that attracted him to Ibn el-Tamaru and other warlords.

From what I gather, Christo Mercer was no Tamburlaine himself, although once, briefly, he'd imagined he was. Mostly, it seems, he modelled his life on the minor character Valdes from the play considered Marlowe's masterpiece: *Dr. Faustus.* As Valdes encouraged Faustus, so did Christo Mercer feel he was aiding his real-life Tamburlaines. That Faustus signed a contract with the devil and Tamburlaine became committed to a life of gore were ironies that I assume would not have escaped him. Especially when he considered the death of the four virgins.

Although they aren't mentioned in his monograph, they troubled him sorely on that mild Thursday night in October 1994. Just as I must admit they amaze even my hardened late-twentieth-century sensibility. The speed with which the virgins were killed is breathtaking. So is the quickness with which Marlowe got them out of the text. And then comes the astounding temerity of Tamburlaine's love speech. It's bizarre. More than bizarre, it's audacious, beyond even Tarantino.

TAMBURLAINE: Ah, fair Zenocrate, divine Zenocrate!
Fair is too foul an epithet for thee,
That in thy passion for thy country's love,
And fear to see thy kingly father's harm,
With hair dishevell'd wip'st thy watery cheeks;
And, like to Flora in her morning's pride
Shaking her silver tresses in the air,
Rain'st on the earth resolved pearl in showers
And sprinklest sapphires on thy shining face,
Where Beauty, mother to the Muses, sits . . .

... And so on (and no, I don't share Christo Mercer's enthusiasm for Marlowe) for another forty-seven lines. But how can he write such poetry after he's had those girls butchered and their "slaughtered carcasses" hoisted on Damascus' walls? This stunt defies the imagination.

Here I picture Christo Mercer putting the book down and going to the window. In his obsession he has forgotten the Englishman's e-mail. He sees Scorpio is rising in the heavens. He looks down at his own garden. The lights in the swimming pool are on and the water is as pale a blue as that over the reefs of Mauritius. About him the house is quiet. In their bedroom his wife is asleep. In their pink bedrooms his daughters are asleep. It is ten past four. Somewhere a dog barks.

"How could you do it, Christopher Marlowe?" he asks of the darkness. "How could you do it?"

8

These days, that is not the sort of question for which you can find an answer. In fact it's been unanswerable since Ingram Frizer stuck a knife into Marlowe's right eye with the "brains coming out on the dagger's point" on the evening of Wednesday, 30 May 1593.

But to get to this murderous detail I have to acknowledge the help of the impeccably CV'd Professor Richard Khafulo, BA Hons (Fort Hare), MA (Oxon), PhD (Columbia), without whose assistance, I must admit ("You will, of course, give me all due credit won't you, Mr. Poley!"), so much of what he has called my "little project" would have remained unilluminated—to use an expression of his. As in: "It is literature that illuminates the soul."

I must state, too, that it is in response to his unintended challenge, even more than my own curiosity and the force of my unfortunate circumstances, that I decided to embark on this "little project." But for his disdainful "Oh, dear!" when I told him that I earned a living writing thrillers, I might've stuck to what I do best.

However.

When in the course of my research—on Wednesday, 13 September 1995, to be precise—I found I needed a quick briefing on the life, work, and times of Christopher Marlowe, I went to the logical place: the Department of English at the University of Cape Town, and there was referred to their latest affirmative acquisition, the ebullient professor.

"Mr. Poley," he said, "you've come to the right man. I've been studying the Elizabethans for more than thirty years in some of the best institutions in the world, while waiting for our former regime, now so gloriously vanquished, to renew my passport."

From Professor Khafulo I learnt that down through the centuries Marlowe's murder had been treated as a drunken barroom fight over who would, or who would not, pick up the tab.

"Which is taking the concept of the English gentleman to ridiculous extremes, don't you think, Mr. Poley!"

In the immediate aftermath another story did make the rounds in London, and this was that Marlowe had died in a fight over some rent-boy.

"Tempting and salacious, Mr. Poley, although unlikely despite Marlowe's predilections in this regard. Rough trade has its irresistible side, hasn't it? But I don't think we should blame the boys for every dastardly deed. No, I think you should view this malicious story as a clumsy attempt at obfuscation. Such slanders are constantly put about by governments trying to discredit their opponents. It is better to see Marlowe as a casualty of political intrigue between Sir Walter Ralegh and the Earl of

Essex: another death in the labyrinth of Elizabethan espionage. You must remember they were all at it in those days: spying, betraying, torturing, murdering. It's how the poets and play-wrights earned a living."

Whatever.

The ghost of Christopher Marlowe that I have Christo Mercer rhetorically addressing seems to have been a minor spy, an atheist (at the time a dangerous nonbelief), a man unintimidated by violence (he was twice involved in violent public clashes, yet never killed anyone), and a playwright given to writing some particularly violent plays.

"Consider, Mr. Poley, how Marlowe has the poor King Edward II put to death by having a red-hot poker inserted in his anus and pushed up to his heart. As can be imagined, 'his crie did move many . . . to compassion.'

"Or there is Faustus' corpse 'all torn asunder,' or the mad orgy of slaughter—his daughter, his daughter's lover, and others—indulged in by the rich Jew, Barabas, who is finally killed in one of his own traps in *The Jew of Malta*. Or there are the bodies that litter *The Massacre at Paris* before one even considers the blood-shed, treachery, and unbridled ambition of Tamburlaine."

For the record, *Tamburlaine the Great* was the first of Marlowe's plays to be produced (in 1587), and it did so well that in true Hollywood fashion he immediately wrote a sequel.

But as it is Part I of *Tamburlaine* that fascinated Christo Mercer, and as Part I is, according to the good Professor, a play of "conquest ending in a temporary 'truce with the world,'" the relevant moral question is: did Marlowe (and, by extension, Christo Mercer) support unbridled empire building or, to again quote Professor Khafulo, "rampant titanism"?

Certainly Tamburlaine is a peasant—a shepherd—who stirs up a private army that goes on a rampage, decimating cities and countries until he is warlord of more than he surveys. Given this, the answer appears to be: yes, both Marlowe and Christo Mercer do appear to have a special affection for imperialistic tyrants powered by bloodlust.

But I am no literary critic and hardly up to answering such an intricate textual point. Professor Khafulo, on the other hand, is: "Really, Mr. Poley, I can find no evidence in the play that Marlowe has any wholehearted admiration for titanic ambition, although I must point out that he is contemptuous of weakness. This is especially true of cowards who won't admit their fallibility. Perhaps I can even postulate here that this is why he has Edward II skewered to death on that 'hot spit.' Wouldn't you agree?"

I nod.

"Mr. Poley," he says, giving me a large smile that creases his eyes, "after my time at Columbia I'm no longer used to this English formality. May I call you"—he glances at my card— "Robert? Please do call me Richard."

Hmm.

"Now, as I was saying, Robert," says Richard, "Marlowe loves gross violence. You only have to look at what Tamburlaine does to the Turkish king Bajazeth and his wife, Zabina, when he captures them. He has Bajazeth caged and then toys with him by offering him meat and drink. At first Bajazeth turns his head away and scorns the food, but later he recants. And as soon as he does so, Tamburlaine refuses to allow him to eat. He humiliates him. He plays with him. He teases him further. Such indignities Bajazeth can't take. He is driven beyond endurance until he brains himself against the cage. When Zabina finds him dead she screams, 'Hell! Death! Tamburlaine! Hell!'—and similarly smashes herself to death against the bars."

This is gruesome. Even against the standards of *Pulp Fiction*, this is stomach-curdling.

But then, like his hero, Christo Mercer was a killer. As a young man he'd spent so much time being trained to kill, been told so many times that he was *going* to kill, that he was hardly surprised when it happened. On the sweltering afternoon of Thursday, 20 November 1975, Jorge Morate stepped out of a bush and Christo Mercer fired five semi-automatic rounds into his chest.

After the ensuing firefight, Christo Mercer saw other men in his unit wandering around dazed by the horror they'd wrought, some even down on their knees vomiting, but he merely went back to the corpse and searched through the dead man's pockets until he found a document of identification. Though he couldn't read Spanish, he could understand enough to know that Jorge Morate had been born in Havana on 26 January 1956. Rifleman Christo Mercer, who was two years older than the Cuban, didn't know the name of the Angolan village his platoon had just decimated, but it did seem to him a long way from Havana. He couldn't imagine why this man would want to come here to fight someone else's war.

Christo Mercer killed a number of people in the bush war. He was on the border from November 1975 until March 1976, and then again from June to September of that year. He did what he was ordered to do. And what he was ordered to do was kill. He shot men during skirmishes. He walked into villages and shot pigs and chickens. He shot fleeing women and children as they waded through the river that was the border between war and peace. He shot elephants for their ivory. After Jorge Morate, he never again wanted to know the names of his victims. Each death had its dream. The horror for him was in his head, at night.

Christo Mercer read only one book during his tours of duty on the border: *Tamburlaine the Great.*

Our quivering lances, shaking in the air,
And bullets, like Jove's dreadful thunderbolts,

Enroll'd in flames and fiery smouldering mists,
Shall threat the gods more than Cyclopian wars . . .

When the rain lashed down in its sudden fury from the towering thunderheads, Christo Mercer lay on his stretcher in the
tent he shared with three others and pictured Tamburlaine
besieging the mighty city of Damascus. When the heat was so
solid they couldn't move and the platoon was strung out in the
shade of the white thorn trees, Christo Mercer was on the
desert plains of Persia. When the mortars shrieked and bel-
lowed about the camp at night in their search for flesh and
blood, Christo Mercer waited in the darkness and heard the
voice of Tamburlaine whisper to him: "Not all the curses which
the Furies breathe shall make me leave. . . ."

9

I re-create.

On the morning of Friday, 7 October 1994, in track suit and
Nikes, Christo Mercer watched the sun rise. He stood on the
lawn in front of the house and watched it come out of the
jacaranda trees. He held a mug of fresh coffee. The Alsatians,
Dingaan and Chaka, whined beside him on the dewed grass. He
was tired. He had just received another e-mail from NS. It read:
"Don't patronize us, Christo."

This implies a response to NS's request for "soothing words."
While there is no record of whatever e-mail Christo Mercer
sent, in order to provoke such an irritated rejoinder it must have
been curt.

The suburb was still: neither traffic nor human sounds.
Suddenly a pair of hadeda ibis went shrieking out of their roost,

and beneath the cries he could hear the brush of their wings. They flew off, their calls becoming less insistent, less urgent. Christo Mercer listened to their passage across the trees, then, abruptly, sharply sluiced the contents of his mug over the lawn: a steaming brown stain. He rushed inside and up to his study.

The smiling icon was leaping about the screen of the laptop. He tapped the space bar. And then he sent a different message to the Englishman.

That done, did he smile? Did he lean back in his chair and stretch? Or did he frown, shake his head in annoyance, and try to dismiss these impinging details? Or did he go back to dreaming about the four girls?

On the basis of what is in "virgins.txt" I must assume he pushed aside reality and contemplated his replay of the siege of Djano. The Gouverneur has summoned everyone to the casbah. He wants four girls to face the wrath—more exactly, the guns—of Ibn el-Tamaru. He is asking for volunteers.

Christo Mercer visualized the throng packed between the mud houses, with the Gouverneur dressed in a dark suit and tie, standing on a cart. The sun was barely up, so it was cold in the shadows. Next to him would be the mullah, and gathered around the cart the town's councillors. The mullah would speak first, calling for God's guidance and mercy and gracious reward in the life after death for those who sacrificed themselves on behalf of their fellows. The Gouverneur then would say all he wanted was four girls to act as emissaries of peace.

"We want you to ask for his mercy. You can tell him that no one will resist him. We will open the gates. We will throw out our guns. The town is his. All we ask is that there is no bloodshed. No killing. You can tell him that we, myself and the councillors, will leave. We will go anywhere, to Paris, Egypt, Ethiopia, it doesn't matter. We will not cause him any problems. He can walk in here, right into my office, and we won't do anything to stop him. Because above everything we do not want there to be any killing. We do not want innocent people to die."

How they would have chanted his praises: Gou-ver-neur, Gou-ver-neur, Gou-ver-neur, Gou-ver-neur!

At that point Gali probably would've stepped forward, her throat choked with sentimentality, her heart pounding. Through tears of pride her mother likely would have been assessing the chances of a cash disbursement in reward for this bravery. But Christo Mercer could imagine nothing that would have prompted the other three to sacrifice their lives. Nor could he see Farida's father allowing his beautiful daughter, a prospective *Vogue* face, to go out and (almost certainly) be shot to death. Many more words must have been spoken. Much shouting. Prayers from the mullah. Simpering pleas from the Gouverneur. A burst of inexplicable gunfire from the bandits. The explosion of a grenade down in the wadi near the well. Then, in haste and confusion and turmoil, it must somehow have ended up that Farida, Dirie, Gali, and Salma were pushed out of the gate clutching a note of surrender that would have meant nothing to the bandits even if they'd allowed the girls to deliver it, because they wouldn't have been able to read the words.

And the girls walked towards the bandits and the bandits duly shot them: Farida, Dirie, Gali, Salma, jerking and collapsing, going down beneath the bullets.

Agitated, Christo Mercer got up and went to run a bath. He lay in water so hot that his flesh turned pink, and put his face below the surface and could hear nothing but the beating of his heart. He lay there for long moments without breathing. He thought of the bodies of the four virgins pinioned to Damascus' wall. He thought of the bodies of the four girls lying outside the town of Djano. He concentrated on these images although he knew that behind them Damascus and Djano were being sacked. People were dying. Women were being raped. Children ran screaming through the streets. Flames took hold in buildings. Smoke turned the light orange. He saw a woman weeping before the bodies of the virgins.

"Christo!" Through the mayhem came his name. "Christo!" And a hand grabbed at his shoulder pulling him sideways. He turned and in a blur of water saw his wife. "Christo, lewe hemel wat maak jy! I wish you wouldn't do that. You look as if you're dead."

"I'm not," he said. His long face was more mournful than ever, his hair stuck to his head like sea grass. "I'm resting," he said.

"You haven't slept."

"I'm never going to sleep again," he replied, and slipped once more beneath the water.

"Christo, please, tell me what's wrong."

He stared up at his wife. The water softened her. She even seemed to be smiling, although he knew she wasn't.

"You're acting very strange."

He pretended he couldn't hear her.

"Asseblief, Christo. Asseblief."

Then she was gone. And from a great distance came the bang of the bathroom door closing, like a mortar exploding in thick sand.

He surfaced to breathe; inhaled; submerged. The bathroom door opened. From under the water he gazed at his daughters giggling over him. To them his face was huge and swollen, his eyes bulged, the thin wisps of hair floated across his balding dome as if unattached to his scalp. When Emily grabbed for his nose, he rose spluttering and shaking off water like a dog. The girls shrieked. Christo Mercer held his enormous face towards them and puckered his lips. Olive and Emily kissed him goodbye, then ran out of the bathroom screaming that they were already late for school. He heard Wilma start the car and drive away.

And then Christo Mercer fell asleep. He did not mean to, but in the moment of silence when nothing moved in the house, he closed his eyes and slept for long enough to dream that he was standing beside Farida's wailing father and the others lamenting over the bodies of the girls. Gali's mother poured sand on her head; Dirie's mother was streaked with her daughter's blood. Someone—he couldn't see the person, it was just a voice—told him Salma's mother and father were dead. And where is Salma? he asked. She is still alive, said the invisible person, whose arm somehow pointed through the crowd. There, that woman's carrying her to find a doctor. But Christo Mercer couldn't see anything. Someone, he realized, had tied a cloth over his eyes. He woke and lay unmoving, to let the dream recede.

"Jesus," he said. "Hell hath no limits."

He closed his eyes again, and this time he could see the woman walking with the prone body in her arms.

Cockatrice, he said to himself. But did I dream it? Was I asleep?

He sank beneath the waters. A vision or a waking dream? What did it matter, since Christo Mercer suddenly knew he was going to die. And every time he closed his eyes, he saw the woman carrying the girl's body.

Who are you? he wanted to shout, realizing that now the dream would reel through his sleep, a closed loop, an unrelenting nightmare from which there would be no escape: nought but blood and war. He hauled himself out of the bath and went to bed. Again he dreamed the dream of the shooting of the girls and it seemed to last for every minute of the five hours he slept.

He woke convinced of grisly death. But who was the woman carrying the wounded girl?

That afternoon, searching through Marlowe's *Tamburlaine*, Christo Mercer found "wretched Zenocrate" walking, in anguish and grief, along the streets of Damascus that were

... strow'd with dissevered joints of men
And wounded bodies gasping yet for life ...

She went outside the city to mourn at the bodies of the four
virgins. She wept at the sight of the four girls speared to death
by men on horses and then hoisted up to hang on the wall. She
lamented:

Ah, Tamburlaine! wert thou the cause of this,
That term'st Zenocrate thy dearest love?
Whose lives were dearer to Zenocrate
Than her own life ...

That afternoon, when Christo Mercer checked his e-mail,
there was a message from the Englishman that simply carried
the image of a skull and crossbones, and beneath it the word
"Nightside."

10

A literary explication: Marlowe's Zenocrate is no Lady Macbeth,
as Professor Khafulo (15 September 1995) has reminded me. She
lacks what he calls "the depth of inner life" that Shakespeare
would have given her. Rather, she is simply a "foil" for
Tamburlaine. If he is rampant power-mad evil, she is goodness
and conscience. "But she is not only a moral cypher, Robert.
There is a complexity to her which manifests itself in her inexplicable and unwavering love for Tamburlaine. Unfortunately
Marlowe doesn't exploit this emotion, being more interested in
the warlord, so Zenocrate is left to hover in the background
wringing her hands."
Zenocrate enters the play as early as scene ii of Act I, when

her caravan, laden with jewels and treasures, is captured by Tamburlaine. He immediately starts wooing her by launching into outrageous speeches couched in what Marlowe refers to as "high astounding terms." At one point, after a particularly fulsome list of promises, his henchman Techelles asks, somewhat sarcastically, "What now?—in love?" Professor Khafulo detects in Tamburlaine's response a hint of cynicism, although I don't agree. Some critics, especially academics, can't look at anything straight on; they're always trying to interpret, interpret, interpret, and in that way they miss the point. What Tamburlaine says is:

Techelles, women must be flattered:
But this is she with whom I am in love.

Undoubtedly this is love at first sight, with a vengeance. And so, by the end of Act I—partly because she has no other alternative (she is, after all, a captive), and partly because she is something of a masochist—Zenocrate resigns herself to her fate with a heavy sigh: "I must be pleas'd perforce. Wretched Zenocrate!"

Wretched indeed. Her next appearance is in Act III, scene ii—the previous act is devoted to the warlord's business of spilling blood—where despite a sadness at her fate she has clearly fallen for her "lordly love, fair Tamburlaine." From here on she is foursquare behind him. Not merely in love, she has also taken to idolizing him, declaring that she wouldn't even believe Mahomet if he personally came down from heaven to tell her that her royal lord was dead.

"None of this is very convincing, Robert, so we have to suspend our disbelief, a concept I'm sure you're most familiar with."

Zenocrate's devotion renders her as captive as a slave. She is utterly powerless. When the taunting of the Turkish king Bajazeth begins, she doesn't intervene or in any way try to curb

Tamburlaine's excesses. She can't prevent the sacking of Damascus—a city within her father's, the Soldan of Egypt's domain. And she certainly can't prevent the death of the four virgins.

But she can lament it all. Hers is the voice of remorse. She bitterly regrets the wanton destruction, the maiming, the loss of life. She would be the first person to stand up before a Truth Commission and confess to her sins of omission:

> . . . pardon me that was not mov'd with ruth
> To see them live so long in misery.

If any of the four virgins had still lived Zenocrate would have been forever stricken with remorse, with guilt, with the need to make good.

It is at this point, I like to believe, that Professor Khafulo's "beauty of literature" revealed for Christo Mercer the bones of his past.

II

Finally, on Sunday morning, 16 October 1994, Christo Mercer wrote in his book of dreams: "I dreamed again of the girls and screamed so loudly it woke Wilma. She said I was thrashing about the bed. She got me to turn over and I went back to sleep immediately. Later in the night I felt her stroking my arm. In the morning she said I was shuddering badly and she had to quieten me."

Christo Mercer flew Kenya Air to Nairobi on Monday, 17 October 1994. At Nairobi he changed planes and flew Sudan Air to Mogadishu. The next day he left Mogadishu for Malitia. He was one of only five passengers on the eight-hour flight west into the blue vastness of the desert.

PART II

Development

12

To begin at the beginning.

My "little project" started (thankfully, because at the time any and every distraction was welcome) on Wednesday, 9 August 1995, when Justine brought round my mail. She knocked on the door; I opened; and she threw the letters in my face.

"I'm not your bloody postman," she yelled. "Get your address changed."

She glanced past me into the mostly empty flat. "Hell, Robert, you're pathetic. It's no wonder I've got your mother on my back."

She glared at me with that how-could-I-ever-have-married-you look of pure, unadulterated disdain. "Accept it, Robert. The sooner you do, the easier it'll be for all of us. And while you're soul-searching you'd better do something about seeing Matthew and Luke. Luke especially."

With that she went flouncing down the stairs.

I made the finger sign behind her back.

Luke, I'll admit, was then, is still, a problem.

Whatever. However.

Among the letters she'd so kindly brought was a slip advising me to collect a package too large for delivery. That afternoon I did so, and it turned out to be a laptop computer. Nothing I'd ordered, certainly, nor are computer companies in the habit of supplying me with machines to test drive. Not once have I been approached to recommend a model, or lend my name to advertising one of their products, despite my belief they might profit considerably from this. The way Rolex did from Frederick Forsythe, or Calvin Klein could by attaching an eau de toilette like Obsession to Lord Jeffrey Archer.

Nonetheless.

This particular laptop (I'm not about to plug the brand name) was so well packed that at first I thought it was new. There was no accompanying note. The parcel had been franked in Johannesburg, which was the only clue of origin. Even the faint smell of onions was too elusive for me to swear to categorically.

In the past, when letter bombs were such a regular part of our postal service, I would've been worried. Back then, writers were a constant target for all kinds of unpleasantry. I seem to recall that sometime in the seventies Prime Minister John Vorster thought it within his duty to call the novelist André Brink a moffie because his hair had a wave, or something like that. But for the moment those days are gone, so I was more intrigued than alarmed by the neat grey machine on my desk.

I plugged it in, switched it on, and discovered it contained— apart from DOS and WordPerfect—a single file. This, called "tamburlaine.txt," appeared to be an autobiography, or at least a story narrated in the first person by one Salma, who explains her relationship with a type of "wretched Zenocrate" here named Sarra. There are no dates with which to fix the story, so as Professor Khafulo poetically puts it, "the text drifts in the realm of fantasy." However, I would guess (for reasons which, if they are not already obvious, will soon become so) that it covers a period from about 1970 to 1987. Certainly the former French colonies in Africa were still experiencing in the late sixties the traumas of decolonization, and this account could describe the aftermath of just such an occurrence.

I have come to regard this story as the last dream of Christo Mercer.

For God's sake, there's a couple fighting on the street below my window.

13

My name is Salma. You will find me dressed in red hobbling around the streets of Djano. The red is meant to symbolize all the blood that has been shed here. But to the tourists I am a splash of colour against the mud walls and often they ask to photograph me. I always oblige. I lean on my stick and stare at their cameras. Like abject worshippers they hop about in the dust to find the best angle. They talk at me in their strange languages. They take their photographs of this crippled woman of Djano. In them, they will find, I am always smiling.

They know nothing about me. They would not believe my story if one of them asked me to tell it. Yet when they photograph me, they photograph a part of Djano's history. And they take this history back to France or Germany or Italy or England or America or Sweden, where it lies exiled in the albums that record their lives. Sometimes they pose with me in the photographs, imposing themselves on my history. But they can't see what has been.

They do not see Sarra carrying me across the sand into the burning town. They do not hear her saying, "Salma, you are the horror. You are all the misery of this day."

Nor do they hear her confession of guilt: "While you were a body lost in darkness, I could treat you. Then you were no one. You had no wants or needs. You were without pain, peaceful, a young girl asleep beneath the sheets, your face at rest, unmarked. I could wash the wounds the doctor had sewn, I could care for you throughout the worst. I could feel the life in you and try to bring you back to it. I wanted you to live.

"But when your eyes opened, when you returned to this world, I

couldn't endure it. Your eyes seemed to accuse me. I felt I had done as much to hurt you as Ibn el-Tamaru.

"You lay there with the pain so rigid and obvious in your face. It pulled your lips, you panted, sweated, fixed me with the eyes of a helpless animal. You seemed to plead for death. And I knew you would always be maimed. No matter what I did, your life would always be only this affliction. I could not be faced each day with such a reality.

"I stopped nursing you. Sometimes I came when I knew you were drugged or asleep. I stood over you, sometimes sitting for long hours. You were again the body I could care for. But there was also the possibility that you would wake unexpectedly. That you would cry out for relief. And what, then, could I do for you?

"There was nothing, no medicine that could restore you, heal you, give you back the unscarred limbs, the perfection of your young body. I felt cursed. By you. You damned me with your hopeless eyes, and so I fled.

"For these last four years I have kept away. Purposefully ignored you. Stayed out of your sight. That was easy, yet still you haunted me. I had the servants put you in the yard each day where I could watch you secretly. Year by year I saw you slowly overcome the awful injuries. Your face smoothed with the lessening of the pain; your mouth loosened, your lips filling out as they'd once been.

"From the servants I heard that you'd brought the ibis. I heard them call you a child of hope. But I know there are wounds which never heal. Unseen, hidden wounds. Sometimes their pain is dimmed, sometimes, for years, there is no pain at all. But the wounds have not healed: they wait, bloody and raw. Those I cannot heal, though I can help you learn to accept them. In talking about them, describing them, there is a kind of hope."

Hope?

I saw hope as an ibis.

In the four years before Sarra took me up to the tranquil room, the servants would carry me to a shady place in the yard and arrange me there with cushions. Peacocks picked about in the dust; a zebra came to take sugar from my hand, its muzzle dry and rough against my skin. I was still weak then, unable to walk, and often tight with hurting.

It was here I first saw the ibis. They came like etched shadows from the sky to drink at a water trough the servants filled especially from the well. I felt the wind of their descent and closed my eyes expecting their feathers to brush my face and leave a shiver upon my skin.

When they started using the trough, the servants were overjoyed. The birds, they said, had never before come down in the yard, despite all the enticing songs they had sung. And so they believed my life was blessed. I was the ibis girl who could talk to the sacred birds. If not because I had asked them, why else did they suddenly take to roosting in the pepper tree? Nothing I could say would convince anyone otherwise. For my part I marvelled that this scavenger of the slum streets could be so revered.

Even so, I imagined hope as an ibis: the stark white wings edged in black; the bald black head, scimitar-beaked, black and glistening; the run of red along the under feathers as if it were bleeding continually. And then the pure grace of its flight: thin, ethereal, so different from the poised malevolence of these birds upon the ground.

I once saw three ibis maul a fledgling goose to death, stabbing out its entrails while the victim waddled helplessly before them, wings outstretched, feathers sweeping the dust; and I cried out at their maliciousness. Helpless to chase them off, I had to witness their cruelty and the other's slow death—an experience that brought the pain back. And for days afterwards I lived in its clarity, feeling each breath, each movement of my body as a sharpness between light and dark. I was only my wound: the bullet sometimes held tightly by my flesh; at other times forcing itself deeper inside me. But despite this I chose to depict the ibis in my tapestries.

What the hell are they doing now! He's hit her over the head with an empty bottle. A line of blood's running down her face. She's screaming, trying to wrestle the bottle from him, then it slips from their grasp and smashes. God-alone but these people aren't human!

How to describe. How to tell. This is what Sarra gave me.

She took me from the kitchen and the yard into a high room of morning light and afternoon tranquillity and music from the radio or, sometimes, her records. From here we faced the red dunes, and through the changing day we watched their changing colours; in the blue windy months we saw them shift and build and draw russet curtains across the sky. She played the music of their moods.

It was a back room reached by a twist of stairs. Each time I mounted them they brought a throbbing to my scars. I would go up slowly, pivoting on my good leg, kicking the weak one onto the next step, and thrusting against Sarra in the upwards movement. At times a steel heat seared through my thigh and I would moan at its intensity, biting hard into my lip to keep from crying out. Sarra said nothing in these moments but held me tightly in her arms. We would wait until my gasping subsided; then go on.

Yet this pain was endurable. For the hours of solace I spent with her and the beads, it was a small price. And over the years I strengthened. The stairs were no longer an ordeal.

I remember in the after-agony of first climbing them I stood, heaving and dazed, before a table strewn with beads of every sort and size and colour, hundreds upon hundreds of them. I limped closer a step at a time, fearful that I would collapse against the table and spill the precious hoard. Sarra came to steady me. I reached forward to run my hands across the beads, to feel them roll and stick or slide beneath my palm. I pressed and they pressed smoothly back. I welcomed them with the acceptance of my skin. I cried at this unexpected beauty.

"First you must get to know the beads," she said. "In every way, each one is exceptional, each one unique, each one its own world. Touch, see, understand the essence within them."

I did as she instructed. Picking them up separately, comparing those of ivory with others ground from horn or tooth. Each one as smooth as the rest, yet in their pale shades of yellowness they contained all they once had been.

"Can you feel it?" she said, leaning towards me across the table, her eyes searching in mine. "Can you feel the elephant?" And then she blew out her cheeks in imitation of this beast I've never seen.

I smiled at her earnestness, and she smiled back.

"I can," she said. "I can feel the elephant in this."

She took a bead from among those I had sorted and held it between her thumb and forefinger. "I can see this animal with its heavy tusks moving in a herd across the plains, the dust rising about them. I imagine they follow the smell of water, eager for it in the heat. I can see them pass into the trees at a river's edge and hear them run shrieking to the mud pools. I know their size. I know their grace. And their anger when men hunt them. This tiny circle is not just a bead. It is the animal. It is every day of its life. It is, too, its death."

She gave me the bead, enclosed it in my hand. "Now," she said, "you must sort all these according to kind and colour."

So I learnt how the beads of clay were different from the beads of stone, even though they both shared a substance and contained the heavy solidity of earth. These stones were amethyst, lapis, onyx, garnet, jet.

The iron, silver, gold, and copper beads seemed to hold a seriousness within them. They spoke, I thought, of trade and greed and exploitation. In them was the burden of slaves and the fires of mongers and smiths. My ears rang with the clangour of men wielding hammers. These I used only once in a tapestry.

But the beads of wood, oiled and smooth as satin, seemed to me to stand for goodness and growth; I could sense the years of drought and the seasons of rain that had gone into them. I could feel the storms the trees had withstood, the high gusting winds that bent and snapped the branches and ached in the roots, and the heat that oozed a resin from the bark.

I also cherished the seeds, these lives that hadn't formed. What they might have been tingled at the touch. There was so much possibility in them.

But the glass beads were the most precious, most light. They sparkled, holding inside a depth like the sky. From them I learnt to see the blue within the blue within the blue. From them I discovered the tone of colours.

"But these are the most important," Sarra said, holding out beads made from bone and eggshell. *"Look at the bone bead, so round, so strong, so polished. See how fragile are beads of eggshell. And yet once this shell protected a life. And once the bone bead was part of some animal's skeleton: a goat, a horse, a camel. Alive, and in its bones it collected perhaps pain, perhaps terror, perhaps sickness, perhaps, too, peaceful days when its world was beautiful.*

"There is nothing in these beads that is evil, Salma, just as there is nothing in them that is good. They're just beads. They've no value, yet they're not valueless. They've no meaning, yet in a tapestry they could have so much meaning they could explain anything. They've no emotion, yet can make us laugh or cry. With these beads you could show the evil or quick moments of good. The beads are neither, yet can be one or the other. It all depends on you."

"Salma," Sarra once said to me, *"you know you'll never have children."*

The words came into the silence as we beaded, and could not be reclaimed. They were black in the air about us: drone flies, with the stench of decay on their legs. I knew the reek from my time of unhealed wounds. I had thought never to smell it again. But perhaps beneath the scars this rot still festered.

You will not have children.

In those days I did not think of this. I did not think, you will be alone to your death. I had my pain and my guilt because I had survived and the others were dead. I had the figures that rose up in my nights to shoot me again.

"You've bled too much, Salma," she said. *"It is why you don't bleed."*

I worked on the black neck of the ibis threading beads of burnt bone, beads of jet into the glistening stem. Her eyes were on me.

"I bleed, Salma. I bleed each day, each night. I cannot have children."

The beads clicked on to the string.

"Children are what Ibn el-Tamaru wants," she said. *"Sons. Even daughters. There is no stopping the blood, Salma. Some days it seeps with-*

out pause, some days there is but a spot to remind me. I can't ever forget. Every day I'm cursed. The blood is always there. You will not bear children, it tells me.

"Because of your love for this man, you will not bear children. So am I punished for what he has done. For what he does. I take on his guilt while he plays warlord.

"Here in Djano he has crates of guns. Boxes of bullets by the pallet. You've seen the men he deals with: the American, the Saudi, the German. You've heard their low voices. You've smelt their stale perfume. These men have slept within this house. And there are others I could tell you about, others who bring horn and ivory and go back with guns to Somalia, Burundi, Rwanda, Ethiopia. In this house each exchange was made, is still made. And I allow it. By doing nothing I allow it. There is no end, Salma, to the blood."

For two years we had beaded in that cool room. She'd taught me the expression of pain. Together we had scoured in the markets for beads, haggled their price, triumphed, compromised. We had sat quietly at the windows while she read from ancient tales; we had rested beneath the palms to watch women drawing water from the well. She had given me back laughter. Yet I could do nothing for her. I had no words, no suitable gesture. Before her despair I was mute. I had only the beads. Black beads for the neck of the ibis.

"I could have given him sons and daughters. They waited within me. I know it, yet I am childless. This he can't forgive me. He says I am bleeding the blood of his unborn sons. He says I have murdered them within my womb.

"I'm not allowed to sleep in his bed; I cannot enter his room. To him I am unclean, barren—worse, an aberration. He says I am not a woman. That I have never been. That in me his seed was destroyed, curdled, discarded like waste. My juices gone acid and yellow."

She stirred a finger through the beads in her tray. They scraped along the wood, filling the silence after her voice.

"Do you believe me, Salma?"

It was a whisper. Words in my head rather than words between us. I nodded. She smiled a small smile, forlorn.

"Once he went to other women to get children. Night after night he left me for them. And then when none of those women gave him children he thought I was laughing at him, that I mocked his nightly escapades. But really I cried for both of us."

What the hell? I thought they'd gone away, but now they're back! Their violence is astounding. He has fallen on the pavement; she kicks him in the head.

"Jou ma's se poes," she screams at him.

He manages to grab her foot and she falls against a parked car.

Good Christ, she's pissing herself!

I remember Ibn el-Tamaru returning from one of his absences with such wonderful presents that they spilled through the house. It seemed to take all day for his men to unload the gifts.

My pain was forgotten; her sadness lost in this magic that conjured— by the touch, the dazzle, the smell and taste—far cities, foreign ports, grand palaces, bazaars of dust and noise.

Ibn el-Tamaru adorned us with silver chains and ropes of amber. He had us dress in long shimmering evening gowns.

I limped about in this finery: hobbling without knowing I was, acting a woman I was not, who had lived no moment of my life, who, I imagined, knew the afternoon glisten of the sea and the white flesh of fish in her mouth and carried on her voice the lightness of small bells rung by morning breezes. This woman was free, and so was I.

Sarra and Ibn el-Tamaru were free, too, until breathless we sat, panting, pearled in sweat, still in our foreign clothes, while he told the story of every piece: who had sold it, where he bought it, what it meant.

He held up a cage of tiny blue and scarlet birds.

"They fly in clouds through the forest," he said, "shrieking worse than

monkeys. But these were being sold by a dealer on the roadside. He had tied them by their feet, hundreds of them, and they screeched and flew in a great ball from his pole. The people there eat them. At intervals along the road I came across groups roasting them. They wanted me to try some, but could you imagine eating these?" The tiny birds hopped about their cage like jewels.

From among the masks he lifted one with two faces: the wood yellowed, shining; the features identical, serene eyes cast down beneath wise hoods, the cheeks scarified with the markings of the tribe. He tried to hold it over Sarra's face, but she pulled away in fright and I took it from him. Felt the surprising lightness, smelled a hint of fire. The wood inside was smooth against my skin. I was touched by the flesh of other faces, looked through the holes where strangers' eyes would have looked out.

"Who wore it?" I asked.

"It is Yoruba," he said. "Probably it belonged to a woman who was regarded as the mother of many children. The tribe believed that whoever the mask gazed upon would become pregnant."

He placed a tall wooden bird before us. "Look," he said, standing back.

We stared up at the carving's accusing eyes, round and black. Its great wings flew out; its head loomed down, long-billed over a swollen belly, grinning a grey snigger. Like no bird I had ever seen, it was neither a marabou nor a vulture.

"Those are carved by the Senufo," he said. "They're put in sacred groves where men go to lie with their women."

"It's evil." Sarra shuddered.

As he glanced at her, his hand stroked down the long bill. Then, abruptly, he carried it out of the room. When he returned his playfulness had not changed and, dangling a pouch before us, he made us cup our hands before shaking into them a few white beads and some yellow ones that gave off a lemon fragrance.

"These," he said, picking both a yellow and a white bead from Sarra's hands, "are holy to the women who gave them to me. They wouldn't take anything in return or else the beads would bring unhappiness."

He picked up the yellow one. "These are made from copal, which the women dig from secret pits. The others"—he held the white one between his thumb and finger—"are made from dolphin bone. Each year the dolphins come to die upon the beaches near their village. Before they die, the villagers tend them by splashing water on their skins and singing to them. It is called the time of stillness."

I rolled the glittering beads about my palm. I couldn't imagine dolphins. But I vowed to thread each bead into the white of the ibis' wings, stringing a memory of oceans among the memories of other animals that dreamed there.

That evening the three of us walked through the gardens where ibis had come to roost in the trees. The light was blue. We did not talk. I leaned on Sarra's arm and they went at my pace. In that moment it was enough.

"Voetsak, go away!" I shout. I'm downstairs on the pavement. "All we want is some peace and quiet round here. Go and donner each other somewhere else!" I wave my arms at them.

"We want some bread, master," she says. The blood is now smeared over her face. She smells worse than boiled dogshit.

"If you don't go," I threaten, "I'm going to call the police."

"Just one rand, master," she says, thrusting a hand towards me. Her stench is gagging.

I dig in my pocket and give her a coin; it's actually five rand, but it's in her hand before I realize my mistake.

"Thank you, master. Thank you, master," she says while tugging at her mate, who's staring at me with unfocussed eyes. His face is truly mangled.

I say nothing.

"May the good lord Jesus bless you, master," she says.

They totter down the pavement towards the city.

One evening in the days immediately after he returned with the presents, Sarra and I were walking on the town wall. The stars had started in the indigo; Djano was going quiet at our feet. We had walked here every dusk since his return. He'd seemed happy. He'd shown us which stars he followed across the desert. I remember Sarra had laughed freely at his stories, walking so closely beside him that I was convinced they must be lovers again.

But this night Ibn el-Tamaru was not with us. We leaned upon the wall, with the roofs below us, the darkening dunes beyond. In the slipping light each faded from the pattern of the town.

"He has put the Senufo carving in my room," Sarra said.

"The pregnant bird?"

"The pregnant bird."

I took her arm.

"And he's hung the mask above my bed."

I could feel her against me, trembling. I pulled away from the wall and we went down the steps into the lanes between the shuttered houses where people still lingered in the doorways and spoke their greetings, which we acknowledged silently and slowly went on, my weak foot scraping.

"Before I wasn't frightened of him," she said.

We neared the house.

"He won't hurt you."

"Before I could stare back at him."

"He won't hurt you."

"I'm not sure of that anymore."

We went in, each to our own rooms.

The next morning she was in the high room before me. She sat bent upon a couch, her head clasped between her hands. She looked up neither at the opening of the door nor at its quick closing behind me. Only at my gasp did she raise her face, her eyes those of an animal before slaughter.

She said, "He wants to drive me mad, Salma."

I hobbled towards her, using the table for steadiness. The light was brown, the shutters were still closed, the air so thick it couldn't be breathed.

"I haven't slept," she said. "All night I haven't slept."

I let in brightness and air, moving from one window to the next until the place streamed with it.

"Everywhere in my room I arranged lamps and candles, allowing no dark corner. When one went out I lit another. I wouldn't have any less light. Even so the bird put a weak swaying shadow on the wall. And sometimes the bird seemed to move."

She lay back; with a damp cloth I wiped her face.

"He didn't come, Salma. I waited for him but he stayed away.

"He has the long-billed bird watching me. This is how he punishes those who cross him."

"You haven't crossed him."

"I have. I have denied his wishes."

I squeezed out the cloth.

"I've told him he's not what he thinks he is. And perhaps he is right, that I have killed our unborn sons. Maybe that's why the bird watches me. If I walk from one room to the other, it follows me with its gaze so that its eyes are ready when I return."

"It's not real, Sarra. It's a carving."

"I know. Yet it troubles me still. Behind the mask there are eyes, also. Last night I saw them in the mask, a glint of eyes."

Occasionally throughout the day, Sarra slept while I worked at my tapestry. This ibis challenged and mocked and spread its wings undaunted, red bolting across their white. Its feet broke the oval of the colours that framed it. Staring out of a single eye, its gaze was blue, all-seeing. The profile of its bill was a scimitar in black. Its yellow head glistened. In this bird was the power of beads, of bone, and of ivory, those of rock, glass, clay, metal. Each had its place and charge.

I wanted it finished, as if only then might there be some release for me. Yet the ibis wouldn't be hurried.

To make it required the monotony of sorting, stringing, and weighting each bead against the one before and the one that followed. Care and patience had created it, along with my childhood, the years of agony, those memories of the dead; none of this could be arranged in haste. I worked as the ibis dictated, taken into its world even as it joined mine.

And beside me Sarra slept. Not easily but haunted, shaking, restless. The lids of her eyes fluttered like moths, her lips puckered, quivered at some rushing dream. Her hands were fists that never opened. She woke to the old agitation.

"I can't go there tonight."

I waited.

"I can't go to my rooms."

I returned the beads in my hand to the cluster on the table. "You don't have to. You're not his prisoner."

She took the stone jug and poured water into a basin, sank her hands into the coolness and splashed it against her face, leaving dark stains upon her gown. She didn't dry where the water ran along her cheeks.

"He'll check tonight."

"You're not his prisoner."

"I am, Salma. I have always been. I see that now. Even to love him was only to bind myself more tightly."

All day he was out of the house. And the house sang—high voices in the yard, a clatter of happiness from the kitchen. Even the blue birds called in their cages. The house breathed and sighed. Aromas came to us of cooking meat, cloves, the sweet heaviness of baked bread. Exuding from the walls was the redolent loam of new mud, so cool, so earthy. Without him the house lived.

He came back late in the night. We heard his footsteps along the street; heard him enter; felt the house tighten.

All this time we had waited, Sarra pretending to sleep while I sorted beads to no purpose, hampered by the dull lamps. Now we sat alert, picking out his sounds over our quickened hearts.

We imagined his passage through the house. First to his rooms, where he would pause frowning at the flames from the paraffin lanterns upon the chest, touching the blue vase, the ornamental dagger, listening for anything *unusual. Leaving there to go into the dark hall, perhaps to stand outside my door, where no yellowness showed along the jamb, before crossing to her room, which was black with her absence. Yet not knowing this, so entering and feeling his way through the first room, passing noiseless over the carpets with only a whisper of his robes on the unmoved air.*

In the second room hesitant, trying to define her sleeping shape or catch the sigh of her breath. Leaning forward, rigid in straining to see, annoyed when he cannot make her out, stretching to feel the slope of thigh and leg. But not finding it. Then, alarmed, groping farther, patting at the emptiness yet knowing she has chosen not to be there.

Nor has she been there to leave a warmth or hollow where her body might have nestled in the wait for him. Only a coolness of sheets beneath his hands. And these thoughts as he straightens up: that maybe this emptiness has been in her love, always. Which echoes through him as he rushes for a lamp from his room, fetches it, returns with it, and, holding out the light, has the bird fly at him from the shadows; the mask leer down.

He cried out then, wailing in anger or bellowing like a stricken beast. And the whole house, hearing this, cowered. She gasped: hurt, too, by the hurt he felt.

We listened to his coming, the terror and noise of it driving up the stairs towards our high room. She stood and faced the door. I sat with my unfinished ibis clutched against my body like a shield and waited as I had once before, for the moment when deranged men would reach me.

At such times there is no fear: only what happens. The smashing of furniture and the destruction of tapestries. Tumult as wood splinters, as tables are overturned, as beads scatter, as chairs are broken against the walls. The act of it roars in the ears. There is nothing but fury: the breaking in, the door flung back, and the inexplicable tinkle of glass somewhere behind.

In the clarity of this instant he becomes a statue: his arms are raised, hands wide; his mouth is open, teeth bared. From this the violence proceeds: embroidered hangings are shredded; the beadwork is slashed; the images pour away. We are like cypresses in a desert storm, she and I; we must bend.

In the end he comes for my ibis screaming not words but rage. My shield is torn from me. I see him rend the fabric, see the beads fly loose in an arc over us.

Sarra told me this about the ibis: it is sacred.

"It cannot be touched," she said. "Neither killed nor destroyed in image. Whoever does so is cursed. In my country we believed that the ibis hatched the world and named it. She made letters from the shapes of mountains, the contortions of trees, the sloughed skins of snakes, from the tracks beetles left over the sand. She made words from the sounds on the wind. These she sprinkled about the earth as she flew and they named the places where they fell.

"Yet she had no words for what happened in these places between these animals. She had to wait until events occurred. She had to leave the story to us.

" 'Who you are,' she warned our ancestors, 'will be known by the tales you tell. These I cannot alter. But I shall judge you by them both in this world and the next. Remember my plumage is the light of the sun, my neck is the shadow of the moon.'

"Saying this she flew off, and has never spoken to us since. Thereafter she chose to scavenge among offal, or pick at carrion, or hunt frogs in the swamps, yet she was venerated. Her image was chiselled in stone. She was depicted among kings. She was wisdom. She had the magic of words and writing. All this we have forgotten. We see her as a soiled bird, yet she judges us still."

The room was never made right. The torn tapestries lay where they had fallen, the spilled beads collecting, over the years, in piles against the walls. The broken furniture remained mute testimony about us. We never spoke of that night.

Sometime, not long afterwards, Sarra cleared the beads and broken glass and smashed tapestry frames from the table with a long sweep of her arm. I remember shivering at the heavy drop and sprinkle of the pieces onto the floor: our high room of shadows was still nervous, still apprehensive. She walked around the table kicking the debris clear while I watched from the window, unsure what this sudden activity meant after our days of stupor. For we had been like the numbed victims of horror: eating, sleeping, walking without purpose.

From a corner that had escaped his rampaging she dragged two chairs and placed them side by side at the table. Then she laid out paper and a bottle of ink and an old dip pen with a steel nib.

She looked at me, her dark eyes unblinking, determined. "Come. I'll teach you to write."

I didn't move, for a moment held her eyes, then glanced away.

"Salma."

"There's no point," I replied. "What I write he'll burn."

"Then you will write it again."

"We can't defeat him, Sarra."

"I'm not talking about defeating him. We're not even going to fight him. We're just going to tell what happened."

"It's not going to change anything."

"No."

"Then why bother."

"Because we have to. Because this is the way we are and we have to describe it. Come."

I was petulant. But even so, I hobbled to the table and sat down. Sarra showed me how to hold the pen. She closed her hand over mine and guided it across the page, filling up the space with large, crude, hesitant designs. To each she gave a sound. I looked at my smudged attempts. Despite my clumsiness I could see the beauty of the individual shapes. I could imagine the slow grace of the signs that represent the sounds of our words. Sarra pushed my efforts aside. The blank paper was beneath my fingertips.

"Again," she said.

Day after day we made the signs. Even when I faltered and could not match the letters to her sounds, or formed the signs with less skill than a child, she kept behind me. Patient. Encouraging.

"It's not easy," she would say. "It will take time. But I'll give you as many years as you need."

Or: "Remember the beads. Think of each letter as a bead. The beads strung together made patterns and out of the patterns you made an image. We're doing the same thing. We'll build words and then sentences and the run of the sentences will be your story. But it takes time."

And so it went until I could draw the script boldly rounded, straight-backed, beautiful. Then she made me copy out the story of Ghanim bin Ayyub, the Distraught, the Thrall o' Love. For days I sat reproducing the elegant marks. With each page the mystery deepened: what little I knew was not sufficient. Letters, a few words, the odd name worked out were all the clues I had, and they were not enough. I had to know what I wrote, and daily it became more urgent. Until at last I finished.

I was enchanted by the story Sarra read. Or rather by the script that I had so slowly, painstakingly crafted to convey this magic. I was engrossed by these signs that could conjure such wonderful pictures in my mind.

I could see Ghanim up his tree quivering with alarm, gripping the fronds so tightly that they must have cut into his hands. I couldn't help but laugh out loud at the sight (it was that real) of the love-struck Ghanim licking at Kut al-Kulub's toes as if they were fresh cream, smothering his face in her feet.

I watched Ghanim's disconsolate mother and sister begging in the streets: their clothes threadbare, grey with dust; their eyes were as dead as those of fishes.

My face streaming tears of joy, I cheered with the crowd that celebrated the double marriage and was dazzled by the jewellery Kut al-Kulub and Fitnah wore.

I was the person who wrote Ghanim's story. I sat on embroidered cushions in the library of the Caliph's palace, where for days the only sound was the scratch of my pen upon the paper. Scholars drifted about me on their quiet slippers, a eunuch — was it Bukhayt or Kafur or Sawab?—brought me coffee scented with cardamom. I looked out of our window not at the dunes of Djano, but at the desert hills of Baghdad *with their sparse groves of olive trees and date palms. I had before me the written words that were the stories of other places. In those words, too, I began to store my life.*

They're back. They're standing outside my door knocking on the frosted glass.

"Master," she's saying. "Master, we just want old clothes."

What do they think I am—an aid agency?

I don't respond. Once they know I'm here they'll be worse than ticks. This is ridiculous. How can I let two toothless meths drinkers terrorize me? I shouldn't have to hide in the bathroom of my own flat.

Much changed in the seven years while I learnt to write. Sarra moved into our upstairs room. The door was shut on her bedroom with the Senufo bird and the Yoruba mask and the stumps of the candles she had used to light away their evil. The door was shut on her life up to that moment. She bought some new clothes, new personal items. She would have nothing that had belonged to her before that night.

The room below became an unvisited place the past could not leave. Her bed with the crumpled sheets which Ibn el-Tamaru had torn in his frantic search had remained as he left it. I know this because after her death I went into the room anxious for a trace of her: hair in a brush, a smell in her long-abandoned clothes, a hint of her scent still on the sheets.

I could have found, and did find, all of this in our room upstairs; but I wanted something older, that belonged to our distant days. And there within the heaviness of dust and closed air hung an essence like the sweetness of cloves that drifted from her in the morning. If I stood still it was there, faintly. In her combs were some hairs as dark as those I had brushed loose on the last morning of her life.

I sat on the bed and looked up at the mask. Eyes seemed to flicker behind the empty slits. Across the room, the Senufo bird would not release me from its gaze. As I stared at the carving, imagining its malevolence, the bedroom door opened and Ibn el-Tamaru entered. At first he did not see me. His eyes were slow in adjusting to the gloom, and for a few moments I could watch him undetected. He pushed the door closed.

In seven years I had seen little of Ibn el-Tamaru. Though he continued to live at the house, his life was quite separate from mine and Sarra's.

They've gone. I won.

I know that government people came to see him. They praised him for over-coming the imperialistes, and they enjoyed his hospitality. From the start they made official what he had taken by force. They wanted no trouble. He was, after all, a hero to the people of Djano. He had given them freedom. What business their hero did with strange men did not concern them. That their hero stored caches of guns and ammunition and land mines in his house did not alarm them. They accepted that, along with his henchmen and the occasional disappearance of someone who had voiced any protest. Such disappearances had happened before. In this Ibn el-Tamaru was no differ-ent from the French lackeys and their goumiers before him. The difference was in the nature of his power. He was sudden and he was savage. Nothing was predictable.

Now I almost gasped at the change in him. In my mind he was a giant, a big man. The night he smashed the tapestries, his muscle filled the room. And before that I had always felt he stood immense beside Sarra and myself. Before that I had never truly looked at him. He was the warlord. His size was in his power. But this was a bony man, a withered man who moved in his drab black clothes with the stiffness of a beetle, not, as I remembered, with a heavy surety that made onlookers cringe. And I won-dered at how wrong I had been all these years, and at the image I had built to hide his ordinariness. As had Sarra.

This was not a feared warrior. This was a beaten man. Defeat lay in the slope of his shoulders, in the forward angle of his neck and the twist of his head. This man was not his legend. For the first time I saw someone who was little taller than Sarra had been, and only a head taller than my crooked height. I could have laughed.

But I didn't. For at that moment he stretched out an arm to rest it on the Senufo carving. I saw the fingers slide down the long bill, then they paused. I glanced at his face. His mouth was open in a grimace. He shouted something that might have been Sarra's name and smashed the bird to the floor. I caught my breath, tried to push up from the bed but faltered and had to stumble to my feet. By then he was coming towards me.

We stood face to face.

"You!" he spat.

I flinched but didn't move.

"You should have died, too."

I tried to hobble past him.

He grabbed my arm. "You're not going anywhere."

"Let me go."

He did not.

"Let me go."

"You poisoned her. Over all these years you've poisoned her. Day by day with your snivelling and your martyrdom and your bitterness you poisoned her. I heard her weeping in the night because of you. Because she wanted to take on your suffering. I took her to women whose men were killed, but their stories she heard without tears. I made her cradle orphans. I made her nurse others with terrible wounds. But she could see no suffering in them. You were the only person who had ever suffered. You were all that mattered to her. Sha! Everyone suffers. But no, she didn't care about that."

He gripped harder.

"I shouldn't have let you live. I should not have listened to her. But I was weak, and you poisoned her heart when I was not there to protect her. Such is your hate, isn't it? This is your revenge."

I pulled against his hold, and he released me.

"Well, you will have your revenge."

I turned away.

"I said I would give you your revenge."

When I started towards the door, he did not try to stop me.

"One day you will see me die too. How would you like that, poisoner? You can watch while someone puts bullets in my heart. You can see me writhing on the ground with the last spasms of life, the blood spreading everywhere. That's what you've wanted all these years!"

It was and it wasn't. As much as I hated and feared this man, I had never imagined his death.

"Isn't that what you want?"

His taunting brought from me a blaze of words I had not realized I possessed.

"Yes," I shouted. "It's all I've ever wanted. I want to see you die the way you wanted me to die."

"You'll see that," he said. "You'll see it for the rest of your life."

"When?"

The unexpectedness of my response made him pause.

"Sha." He smiled—a smile of malice that lasted too long, and pulled his lips until they thinned and his teeth showed beneath the fringe of his moustache. He came towards me but this time did not clutch at me. "So you want to know when?" he whispered. "Only Allah knows when."

On the morning before Sarra died, she asked me to brush her hair. She sat on the bench facing the dunes while I performed our slow ritual. Her dark hair sparked and crackled, and each stroke stirred the aroma of cloves. As usual I took longer than was necessary. The motion absorbed us both, entranced us with a sense of well-being. From the radio came quiet music; in the backyard the voices of the servants rose occasionally, sound without words. There was nothing in these moments we had not shared before. And yet for her it must all have been different. Perhaps a clarity such as I had known when the details were noise and bullets and agony. Perhaps a slow inevitability: the sun slipping across the floor, leaving our room to the blue that was its proper colour.

While I brushed she sat without speaking, and it could have been any of the countless times I had done it in the previous years, except it was not.

It was the morning before Sarra died.

All I can say is that we were in the same room for that last morning of her life and I don't know what she was thinking. Sometimes I believe she must have gone into such despair that she was numb. I can think of nothing else to explain it. She must have sat without thought, without feeling. Her emotions had become sand. I run my fingers through sand and imagine each grain a crystallized tear. There was desert inside her: a sand vastness with outcrops of rocks. I shut my eyes and this is Sarra. It makes remembering easier for me.

She came to look at what I had written.

I slid the paper out towards her. Perhaps I shouldn't have let her read it; perhaps it served only to reconfirm the decisions she'd made. In the days afterwards I came to see my fledgling words, the start of my story, as the end of her life. I do not think that anymore.

This is what she read:

They did not hear the groaning of the camels or dogs barking or the shifting of men, how their clothes rustled, the snap of weapons being loaded, being readied; nor could they smell woodsmoke or the food that had been cooked on these fires; they did not warm when the sun came on them as they moved from the shade of the wall towards the black figure and his fighters. They could not feel the desert beneath their sandals. They had none of the senses but sight. And they saw only Ibn el-Tamaru. Not the horde of men armed with the cast-off weaponry of other wars.

There were four of them. They were young. They walked hesitantly, watching to see if he would move towards them. There was one in front and another, slightly behind her, to her right. The two following behind walked closely together, their shoulders sometimes touching. One of these looked round at the town. She saw flashes of sunlight striking on metal or on the glass of binoculars. She saw a man—the Gouverneur?—wave them on, exhorting them, driving them away. She wanted to run back but couldn't. She could only walk as the others were doing, forward, towards him. None of the others glanced back.

Sarra put down the piece of paper. She told me of a terrible fear, an anxiety so powerful she couldn't breathe, that pushed down on her chest like an invisible foot each morning when she woke.

"Often I thought it was Ibn el-Tamaru, that he had come to kill me," she said. "But of course I was alone and it was light so I could see the shapes of things around me.

"I would lie there afraid, imagining how a horde of bats crawled over my heart, beat against my ribs until they escaped between the bones and swarmed up my throat. I tried to retch them out, my whole body heaving to vomit, but I couldn't.

"Each morning started this way. I would get up and do anything to distract myself: move a vase to twenty different places, count out loud so that the numbers echoed in my head. I would crawl along the floor counting the beads until I could hear you on the stairs. Then I knew I was safe again. With you there I could keep the dread away, although sometimes it returned even when we were together.

"Or rather it was always there, and I always had to shut it out. And I knew, Salma, that I couldn't do that forever. Over the years I have come to realize this thing is not fear or anxiety or horror or dread. That might be what it feels like, but it is worse than that. It is despair, Salma. I despair."

A knock, rapid, staccato, sharp like distant machine-gun fire: "Master, please, master . . ."

I cannot imagine the loneliness. I cannot imagine the suffering. I cannot even imagine the pain.

The next morning I found her convulsed by it. She lay curled on the floor. Her face was swollen; her eyes pleaded for release; her lips were stretched into a permanent grimace and bruised. I went to her, horrified. She asked—whispering, barely able to make the sound—for water. Her tongue was shredded. Slivers of glass embedded in it, and in her palms.

I found the jug smashed on the floor where she had clawed it from the table, a stain still damp along the boards. I yelled to those in the kitchen for a bucket of water, while before me, at the agony that racked her, she bit her fingers to stop herself from screaming. I wanted to scream for her myself at this awfulness I couldn't understand.

A servant came up—harrowed, alarmed. I took the pitcher at the door without allowing him a glance inside. What he would have seen was a chaos that looked as if she had been attacked: the bed soaked with bloody vomit, her gown too; the furniture strewn about, chairs knocked over, cushions torn and their stuffing ripped out, balls of cotton drifting everywhere.

I crouched beside her with the water, yet she still wouldn't let me touch her. I couldn't even raise her head. I had to pour the water slowly into her mouth. It made her retch once again, and this time she couldn't help but cry out. And then the pain must have subsided, because she let me wipe her face. She shivered, so I covered her with a rug. She held my hand.

I sat with her all the time she took to die. And for a long while afterwards I sat there whimpering.

At the death of those we love our grief is terrible. It is heavy and hard and with us every moment. Slowly it sinks into our depths, going down with memories and images and dreams to that place in us that is quiet, mournful, blue: a sanctuary of graves of those we were and of those we knew who in all the days remaining we visit, sitting at the stones we have built to honour them, telling our sadness, this sorrow for the lives we live without them.

Note 1: Bloody hell!

Note 2: What was I supposed to make of this? What was it supposed to mean?

Note 3: I was told by Professor Khafulo that the above piece was written somewhat in the style of the magic realists who "incorporate elements of fantasy into what is otherwise a narrative of everyday realism."

"It's a most useful mechanism for dispensing with the trivia of realism when history is the actual subject. You should try it sometime, Robert," he said, smiling so broadly his nostrils flared. Gradually the smile faded, and he added: "Although, to be honest, what we need is to incorporate elements of realism into the everyday fantasy of our lives, don't you think?" (22 September 1995)

The conjunction—his word—of "reality" and "fantasy" was supposed to remind readers of "the invented nature of narratives." And so for this reason I called the story "The Last Dream of Christo Mercer."

Note 4: Of course when I received this exercise in the "disruptive narrative technique of magic realism," I had no idea who Christo Mercer was, nor had I read Marlowe's *Tamburlaine the Great*. In fact, I'd never heard of the Elizabethan play, so the clue in the file name was useless. I went searching through an encyclopedia (*The New Caxton Encyclopedia* of 1969, the only set I possess since Justine has the *Britannica* for our sons, who moreover have the world of CD-ROM literally at their fingertips) for references to a Tamburlaine and found this:

Tamerlane: Mongol ruler and conqueror, also known as Tamburlaine and Timur Lenk or "Timur the Lame" (c. 1336–1405). Like his forebear Genghis Khan, Tamerlane was a brilliant conqueror and ruthless warlord who established a vast but short-lived empire in central Asia. The tornado-like nature of his career has left a legendary reputation in the West, which found full expression in Christopher Marlowe's play *Tamburlaine the Great*.

"The Prince of Destruction," as Tamerlane was aptly called, began his career when he succeeded his father as a minor Turkish chieftain in 1360. After defeating the khan of North Khorasan and Jagatai in 1369, he overcame opposition in Persia. From his capital at Samarkand, Tamerlane attacked both East and West. His hordes reached Moscow in about 1381, and then towards the end of his life he made for the Middle East, taking Smyrna and Ankara and defeating the Sultan Bajazet I in 1402. (This westward pressure incidentally relieved the Byzantine Empire by forcing the Turks to end their siege of Constantinople, thus extending the capital's life for another fifty years.) Between these attacks on the West, Tamerlane had overrun India in 1398, leading his armies in the sacking of Delhi. After his successes in the West in 1402 he planned to take on the Chinese Empire, but died while marching his armies eastwards.

Despite the pointer here to Marlowe, the pressure of cleaning the flat and moving in (with a mattress and sleeping bag, a cheap pine desk and hard kitchen chair for furniture, the second-rate encyclopedia for decoration) prevented me from reading the play immediately.

From one perspective I was fascinated by the mysterious arrival of this laptop computer and its story, but I could deduce nothing much from either one. From another perspective the above story was little more than a fantasy about a guilt-stricken woman's despairing path to suicide. Albeit a particularly agonizing suicide! According to my friend, the poet and doctor Phil du Plessis, eating slivers of glass is an appalling way to die. Which seems to me to be taking atonement to perverse extremes, but then the poet Ingrid Jonker chose to drown herself over the inequities of apartheid—or, at least, that's the political version of her suicide. I suspect she was also a psychological mess.

Thus, given the imponderables, I decided the best course was to quieten my curiosity and wait. My theory was that an aspirant writer (probably someone presently in advertising) was indulging in flamboyant measures to get his work read. (I am plagued by such aspirants seeking free reassurance about their pathetic efforts.) In due course, I was sure, a letter would follow to explain the ruse.

Note 5: Click on some definitions:

i. Justine: a wife; my wife.

ii. Wife: from the rack of dictionaries in the Cape Town City Library, this interpretation in *The Concise Oxford Dictionary of English Etymology* (OUP, 1987) of the word "wife" will do: "woman (surviving in *fishwife* . . .); woman joined to a man by marriage."

iii. Fishwife: "an abusive woman"—which she is, with a vengeance—"who . . . guts fish"—which is what she's doing to me with a sharp and ruthless knife. (Those explanations from *The Longman Dictionary of the English Language*.)

iv. Marriage: "1.a., the mutual relation of husband and wife; the state of being husband and wife. 1.b., the customary practice whereby a man and a woman are joined in a special kind of social and legal dependance" [*ibid.*].

v. Divorce: "*n*, a decree declaring a legal dissolving of a marriage"; "*vt*, 1.a., to end marriage with (one's husband . . .); 1.b., to dissolve the marriage between (husband and wife)" [*ibid.*].

vi. Depression: "*n*, a state of feeling sad; dejection" [*ibid.*].

vii. Dejection: "*n*, lowness of spirits." But as an adjective it's a better diagnosis: "cast down in spirits," from the Middle English "dejecten": "to throw down"—which is [*ibid. ibid. ibid.*] what it feels like.

However. Whatever. Onwards if only sideways!

viii. Moffie: "Homosexual, sometimes a male transvestite"—from *A Dictionary of South African English* (OUP, 1991).

But there's more, there's more. In fact there's a whole entanglement here with our dark and insulting past because in that Bible of the Taal, the *Handwoordeboek van die Afrikaanse Taal* (Voortrekkerpers, 1965; edited by P. C. Schoonees, C. J. Swanepoel, S. J. du Toit, C. M. Booysen), it's stated that "mof" was once used as a derogatory term for an Englishman. It can also be used to describe someone who is drunk, although it admittedly is most commonly used with reference to a half-breed animal—particularly where an indigene was penetrated by an imperialist import. So "moffie" is less a simple word than loaded baggage. "Mof," by the way, can also mean a muff or mitten. My theory is that "moffie" has come about because we have a propensity (maybe common to all colonizing cultures) to diminish or tame everything. A moffie sounds less terrifying than a mof. Finally, in the *Tweetalige Woordeboek* (Tafelberg, 1984; edited by D. B. Bosman, I. W. van der Merwe, L. W. Hiemstra), whose arrogant title implies that only those who speak Afrikaans and English can claim to be bilingual, a "moffie" is defined as a nancy boy, pansy boy, queer, or fairy.

ix. "Jou ma's se poes" translates as "Your mother's 'n, slang (obscene). The female genitals'" (*Dictionary of South African English*). Although this sounds like the ultimate curse, it carries no more invective than a mild "damn" among bergies.

x. "Donner" is an alternative spelling for "donder," which in *ibid.* is rendered as "to beat up, thrash." Somehow neither of these explanations quite gets the measure of a word that contains thunder and lightning. There's nothing less than God's wrath clashing about the skies in here.

xi. Bergie: "A vagrant living usually on the slopes of Table Mountain, Cape Town" [*ibid.*]. In my case, vagrants (plural) living frequently in a cardboard box in the stairwell of Victoria Court.

xii. Goumiers: "irregular native troops ... whose renown was later to extend far beyond the Sahara to make them one of the most feared and formidable elements of the French army. Volunteers, they served when they liked and for as long as they liked. The French authorities would provide them with sabre, rifle, bayonet, and cartridge-belt, and pay them a monthly wage. . . . [F]or a desert tribesman, to join a goum meant to gain security without sacrificing his cherished way of life, his independence or his freedom" (John Julius Norwich, *Sahara*).

xiii. Luke: a son. Fourteen years old. Arrested two days ago with enough dagga in his pockets to make him a drug baron. I can't deal with this.

Note 6: In this time of remembering (especially with so much of it coming from the Truth and Reconciliation Commission) we have to get our facts straight, even the most trivial ones. So let it be known that John Vorster didn't call André Brink a moffie—that story's been fabricated by the popular imagination. The actual story, the basis of the myth, according to André Brink: "You may recall in the early seventies the police broke up [with the normal paraphernalia of dogs, batons, water cannons, and viciousness] a student demonstration in Cape Town, and some of the students took shelter in St. George's Cathedral. You may remember, too, that the police went in and beat them up in the church and arrested them. In response to this I wrote to Vorster in protest, pointing out to him that this was worse than de Gaulle's handling of the student protests in Paris in the late sixties. I also reminded him that shortly afterwards de Gaulle was out of a job. Then I wished him a good night's sleep. He wrote back to say my comments were exactly what he expected from a pinko-liberal. He fumed on for a bit then he wished me a good night's sleep and hoped the pillow wouldn't mess up my hair curlers" (Personal telephone interview: Thursday, 18 January 1996).

Note 7: "This is most interesting, my dear Robert," was Professor Khafulo's comment when I asked him about the reference to the story of Ghanim, etc. "What we have here is a classic example of the invidious way in which the colonizing culture writes itself onto the invaded culture. These people—this Salma and her friends—are Africans; they have their own stories, their own oral tradition, and yet that has been usurped completely. In its place the French gave them the *Arabian Nights,* because that is how the French understood their African colonies. Africa, Arabia—all the same. It was the Other. So Sarra's favorite story issues not from her own historical narrative but from an import.

"This is most distressing, and an example of how thoroughly invasive and destructive occupying cultures are—just one instance of the many I have personally encountered. You'd be amazed, I'm sure, to know there are cafés in Abidjan, Dakar, and Rabat that you'd swear were transplanted lock, stock, and barrel from the Boulevard St. Germain. Admittedly, sometimes one is thankful for these tender mercies. But that is not the point. The point is the degree to which the native—I use the word in its proper sense—to which the native culture is negated. Nay, obliterated."

Note 8: The story of Ghanim bin Ayyub, the Distraught, the Thrall o' Love can be found in Richard Burton's *Book of the Thousand and One Nights* (London, 1958), which is his rendition of the *Arabian Nights.*

"These stories are based on oral techniques of interwoven narratives" was how the Professor explained "the underlying structure" of the tales. "The subtext in this instance, Robert, is sexual superiority. The feminists would say this is a story about men, their violence, their guilt, their hatred of women, and the misery we bring to the sisters, the sad things we make them do, and the gratitude they wallow in when we smile at them.

"It is, as you will see, a love story where the lovers are plunged into awful despondency but from which they are rescued by a happy ending. Love, loyalty, and trust triumph one and all. The story is complete, unlike the story of our lives. The feminists would hate it."

Whatever.

Ghanim's story is too long to include here, though for the curious I will go to the trouble of supplying this expurgated retelling.

My version starts on the night that Ghanim bin Ayyub is hidden in the fronds at the top of a date tree, listening to three black slaves—Bukhayt, Kafur, and Sawab—tell of their castrations. This palm tree is in a graveyard outside the walls of Baghdad; the slaves are resting beside a heavy chest they have carried out of the city.

Their stories are laced with words like "pickle" and "pizzle" and the "futtering" of "slits," which inevitably leads to the loss of maidenheads. However, the real story concerns the young lady held captive in the heavy chest who is rescued by Ghanim and smuggled back to his house.

A month and much sexual frustration on Ghanim's part goes by—a consummate cock-teaser, she won't allow him into her trousers—before he learns that she is one of the Commander of the Faithful's concubines.

"My name is Kut al-Kulub—the Food of Hearts," she tells him. "I was the Caliph's favourite, which so angered his wife, the Lady Zubaydah, that when the Caliph was travelling in distant lands she had me drugged and I would have been buried among the tombs had you not rescued me."

The news of her position greatly upsets Ghanim. Though hopelessly in love with her, he knows he cannot touch the Food of Hearts. He broods and weeps and curses his fate until Kut al-Kulub, moved by his distress, decides to put the past behind her and let their love have its way. She takes him in her arms, kisses him, tells him she loves him and is willing to risk anything to be with him. But Ghanim is too awed by the Caliph, too law-abiding and religious to allow this. For three months they live unhappily in an impossible state of longing until one day, while they are eating, Kut al-Kulub looks out and sees the house is surrounded by the Caliph's guards with their swords drawn.

What had happened was this: when the Caliph returned from his travels, Lady Zubaydah told him that Kut al-Kulub had died an untimely death and now lay buried in an honoured place within the palace. The Caliph went into deep mourning and spent a whole month weeping at the tomb. His grief was unbounded and seemingly endless. Perhaps he would never have recovered from his sorrow had he not overheard two of his slaves discussing the real fate of Kut al-Kulub: that she had been staying at Ghanim's house for the past four months.

So now his guards are outside Ghanim's house while inside Kut al-Kulub is dressing her unconsummated lover in ragged old garments so he might slip away disguised as an indigent. Kut al-Kulub says that Ghanim has already taken his goods and gone back to Damascus. The poor woman is whisked away and locked up in a dark room, and Ghanim's house is sacked.

But the revenge of the Caliph does not end there. He is legally allowed to reduce Ghanim's family—his mother and sister, Fitnah—to poverty, which he does. The two women are thrown out of their house and left destitute to face a future, like Ghanim, of wandering the land as beggars.

There follow hard months of sickness, hunger, indignity,

and heartache until Ghanim ends up in the house of a kindly Baghdad merchant who takes pity on him, thinking him a wandering pauper or a man down on his luck.

The two women also drift towards Baghdad, arriving at no less a house than that of Kut al-Kulub, who subsequently has been exonerated by the Caliph when he learnt, by chance, that neither she nor Ghanim has dishonoured him. Kut al-Kulub hears the women's story, knows instantly who they are, and assures them that their days of adversity have ended.

Since her restitution she has been searching the bazaars for Ghanim, her love for him spurring her on. She also has been given the Caliph's permission to marry the Distraught, the Thrall o' Love, should she ever find him. Needless to say, she does; he regains his health; and the Caliph restores him to wealth.

The story ends with a double marriage: Ghanim to Kut al-Kulub; and the Caliph to Fitnah. What happened to Lady Zubaydah is not revealed.

The reason Ghanim's story is known today—or so they say—is because the Caliph ordered that it be recorded and deposited in the royal library so that all who came after him might read it and marvel at the dealings of Destiny.

Note 9: Because the subtext of Ghanim's story is so sexy, and sex sells, and because a copy of the *Thousand and One Nights* is probably not to be found in every home, this (briefly) is how one of the slaves, Bukhayt, came to lose his balls.

As a five-year-old Bukhayt was captured by a slavedriver from a neighbouring African tribe, and sold to an Egyptian who had a three-year-old daughter. For the next seven years the two children played together quite happily—until the day Bukhayt came across the young girl sitting perfumed and lusty in an inner room. According to his account, the girl began playing with him until his pickle stood erect, at which stage she grabbed it and rubbed it "upon the lips of her little slit outside her petticoat-trousers." This was too much for the aroused Bukhayt, who threw his arms around her; and before he knew what was happening, his pizzle split her trousers and entered her slit and took away her maidenhead. At which stage the spent Bukhayt ran off.

The girl's mother learnt of the incident but, out of compassion for Bukhayt, kept it secret. The girl was hastily married off to a barber, and on her marriage night the blood of a pigeon was surreptitiously and symbolically sprinkled on her sheets. Following the wedding Bukhayt was seized while he slept, castrated, and made the girl's eunuch. This meant he had to attend to her constantly, whether at bath or table, a circumstance which played, so to speak, right into their hands.

Naturally their sexual trysts continued. These, Bukhayt boasted to his fellow castrati in the graveyard underneath the palm tree as Ghanim hid in its fronds, she greatly enjoyed because he could sustain his erections for long periods. Being ball-less he was unable to climax. Nor, for that matter, was there any sticky mess at the end.

Unfortunately these stainless years of bliss ended abruptly when the barber died and Bukhayt was bought by a Baghdad merchant.

Note 10: I am the writer, the reconstructor, and the developer. I choose what to include and what to leave out. What follows could have been left out, and I'm including it only in the interests of integrity and truthfulness.

My mother knows Justine and I are no longer living together. She doesn't know why we've separated, though she thinks I'm to blame for what's gone wrong. And I've not said anything to the contrary. She wants me to move in with her until Justine and I have settled our problems. What happens when I go to visit her, as I did for lunch five hours ago, is that she makes me feel like a little boy.

I am six years old. I have been bullied by the class tough. I have pissed myself. I have to walk home in my wet khaki shorts. As the other kids laugh at me, I pretend I am the astronaut Mark Saxon; they are the aliens whom I disintegrate with my ray gun. My mother, alas, is immune to my ray gun.

"Oh Lord, Robby, not again," she moans. "When are you going to stop being such a sissy."

And then, years later: "You can't just run away because you had a little disagreement, Robby. If I'd run away from your father every time we had words, we'd have had no marriage at all."

"I've been married for twenty years, Mom, and this is the first time anything like this has happened."

"I know Justine's got a sharp tongue, but people don't mean what they say in the heat of the moment—and you can be *very* irritating sometimes."

"Irritating! I can be irritating?"

"So I think you've blown this way out of proportion. That's always been your tendency. . . ."

I am, to import a wonderful English expression, gob-smacked.

"You always made mountains out of molehills. No problem was ever too small that it couldn't be exaggerated into something insurmountable. And that's what you've done again. You've been married for twenty years, Robby. You can't just leave at the drop of a hat. And certainly you don't go renting a flat like a poor white. Only poor whites live in town, surely I don't have to tell you that!"

"Mom . . ." This comes out as a six-year-old's whine. I can't believe it.

"Now, what I think you should do—and I've told this to

Justine, too—is forget about the flat and move in here until you can patch things up with your wife. You've got a family to think about."

I am reduced to a snivelling boy in clean shorts standing before his mother, who holds his hand while imparting worldly advice: "There, Robby, it's all better now." A ruffling of my hair, highly annoying. "You know, you're going to have to learn to stand on your own two feet. You can't come running home to Mommy every time you have a fight." A peck on the cheek. "There's a good boy." A smile. "Go on, now. Run along and play."

What chance do you have of being an adult while someone's alive who changed your nappy?

14

On 17 August 1995—about a week after the laptop arrived—I received in the regular mail (no longer hand-delivered by Justine) a stiffy disc containing a copy of Christo Mercer's paper "The Nature of Political Power in Marlowe's *Tamburlaine the Great*" and the "virgins.txt" and "e-pisodes" files. Once again, these missives were unsigned and without an explanatory note. The package had been posted in Johannesburg.

Vaguely irritated at the lengths my hopeful writer was going to in his promotional campaign, I nevertheless played along. Who wouldn't? Curiosity is worse than orgasm: it can't be resisted. Besides, I needed plenty of activity in my new separated life, which had reintroduced me to laundromats, whisky from coffee mugs, and that obligatory feature of all flats in old blocks called names like Victoria Court, the chipped enamel bath. Who needed a pumice stone or a loofah or someone to scrub your back when you had such a bath as this?

"This place is ridiculous" was Justine's opinion of my new abode. "You're trying to live out some adolescent fantasy. You don't have to stay in this dump, Robert. It's not as if you can't afford a Clifton apartment, so if you're doing this to make me feel guilty, forget it. I'm not falling for that trip. I've had enough of your manipulation."

I, on the other hand, couldn't (and can't) see anything wrong in living among Internet cafés, strip joints, old bookshops, nightclubs, mosques, pawnbrokers. This is Long Street. In ten minutes I can walk down a street that is in fact long and be among the city's tower blocks; in twenty minutes I can reach the harbour farther on. I can drink beer among the crowds at Quay 4. I can sit on a bench in the Gardens and watch the skirts ride up the thighs of young women lolling on the grass, or go swimming in the Long Street baths. I can gaze at the prostitutes; I have even learnt to accommodate (the often tiresome) Omar Sharif and Bette Davis.

I like living in Victoria Court. I like to look at the mountain looming through the afternoon's haze of salt. I want to hear the cannon at midday and the rise of pigeons, disturbed by the bang, beating up from the pavements. I want to be woken by the bad fish smell that seeps off the docks after a warm night. I even want the heat in these rooms to make me glisten with sweat. I'm used to the loud blue rush of the wind down the mountain. I've come to set my so-called inner clock by the muezzin's call.

And this is not just bravado in the face of suddenly shattered domestic bliss. I mean it.

So.

So I booted up the laptop, slipped in the disc, and loaded the contents onto the hard drive.

The essay on Marlowe turned out to be a tract at once tedious and tendentious, an argument in favour of the rule of order and its rigid enforcement. This came as no surprise, dated as it was, two years after P. W. Botha made himself a constitutionally invincible State President. This was also the year that Botha declared a State of Emergency throughout the country.

In retrospect, the only material of any note are some quotations from Machiavelli's *The Prince*, and they're of interest only because of what they say about Christo Mercer's mind, at least as it operated in 1987.

For example, he buttresses a discussion of Tamburlaine's rise to power with Machiavelli's assertion that "a prince . . . should have no other object or thought, nor acquire skill in anything, except war, its organization, and its discipline. The art of war is all that is expected of a ruler; and it is so useful that besides enabling hereditary princes to maintain their rule it frequently enables ordinary citizens to become rulers."

Witness P. W. Botha *et al.*

And when examining the need to enforce law and order for the greater good, he turns again to Machiavelli: "a prince should not worry if he incurs reproach for his cruelty so long as he keeps his subjects united and loyal. By making an example or two he will prove more compassionate than those who, being too compassionate, allow disorders which lead to murder and rapine. These nearly always harm the whole community, whereas executions ordered by a prince only affect individuals. A new prince, of all rulers, finds it impossible to avoid a reputation for cruelty, because of the abundant dangers inherent in a newly won state."

I repeat, in retrospect these extracts offer insight and perhaps go some way to explaining why Christo Mercer did what he did. At the time, however, I yawned. As far as I'm concerned, Machiavelli is notable purely because of his low opinion of human nature—probably the single redeeming feature in his political philosophy.

But of course "virgins.txt" is a whole lot more interesting. Representing an awareness of horror, especially when read in juxtaposition to the "Political Power" bullshit, is it not a turning from the grand machinations of politicians and warmongers to the impact of their doings on ordinary lives? Or am I taking it all too far? Interpreting too freely in seeing signs of remorse in Christo Mercer?

At the time I scratched my head and read Marlowe's play, and like Christo Mercer was struck at his treatment of the four virgins. Marlowe must've had Machiavelli perched like a parrot on his shoulder.

Note 1: For those interested, the relevant text (Act V, scene i, lines 119–134):

VIRGINS: O, pity us!
TAMBURLAINE: Away with them, I say, and show them Death!
        [Techelles and others] take them away
I will not spare these proud Egyptians,
Nor change my martial observations
For all the wealth of Gihon's golden waves,
Or for the love of Venus, would she leave
The angry god of arms and lie with me.
They have refus'd the offer of their lives,
And know my customs are as peremptory
As wrathful planets, death, or destiny.
        Enter Techelles
What, have your horsemen shown the virgins Death?
TECHELLES: They have, my lord, and on Damascus' walls

Have hoisted up their slaughter'd carcasses.
TAMBURLAINE: A sight as baneful to their souls, I think,
As are Thessalian drugs or mithridate:
But go, my lords, put the rest to the sword.
                    Exeunt [all except Tamburlaine]

Note 2: Professor Khafulo finds it significant that *Tamburlaine* doesn't open with the man who aims to be the "scourge and wrath of God" but with the "weak, petulant, and effeminate Persian King Mycetes." He argues that while Tamburlaine is ruthless, Mycetes is morbidly cruel. Which is why Mycetes longs to see his milk-white horses adorned with severed human heads:

And from their knees even to their hoofs below
Besmear'd with blood, that makes a dainty show.

Professor Khafulo comments: "As you can see, this brilliant opening portrays a morally bankrupt world corrupt to the point of hopeless decadence. Into this comes Tamburlaine with the presence and energy of the archetypal Noble Savage. We could, if so inclined, draw analogies with our present situation, don't you think? And then we would be able to understand why the Elizabethans couldn't help but admire this man Tamburlaine, who knows what he wants and the road to it."

Note 3: On Elizabethan jingoism, Richard Khafulo PhD (Columbia) has this to say: "For the Elizabethans, Mr. Poley [this was before the Robert bit], Tamburlaine was a manifestation of power. That explains the play's popularity. Here was a man who bestrode the world. They liked that. You just have to hear the energy, stridency, and bombast of the verse to realize that it's meant to rouse people to a patriotic fever pitch. [He flicked through his copy of the play.] Here, what about this:

> If thou wilt stay with me, renowned man,
> And lead thy thousand horses with my conduct . . .
> Those thousand horses shall sweat with martial spoil
> Of conquered kingdoms and of cities sack'd.

'Of conquered kingdoms and of cities sack'd,' Mr. Poley: Tamburlaine is a megalomaniac, but how the Elizabethans applauded him.

"He appealed to the latent imperialism that was rising up like a foul vapour in the nation—to wit the voyages of Ralegh and that other pirate, Drake. Believe me, Tamburlaine marks the beginning of English expansionism as a cultural expression. Most alarmingly, it issues a particular warning to Africa. Consider this, Mr. Poley:

> Do not my captains and my soldiers look
> As if they meant to conquer Africa?

And then, not fifty lines farther on:

> But, as I live, that town shall curse the time
> That Tamburlaine set foot in Africa.

What does this indicate if not colonial designs? Is it any wonder that not many centuries later the British would turn almost all of Africa into their dominion? It's right there in the Elizabethan age that the roots of imperialism took hold. Just look at them. The English were already causing problems in Ireland, and soon they'd be out trampling all over the world. It wasn't so many years later when they first set foot in India" (13 September 1995).

Note 4: Because of his nose and her eyes I call my bergie couple Omar Sharif and Bette Davis. They call me Mr. Gentleman Robert. So far, for the honour of this title, I have paid a small fortune in cash and donated food and even a bottle of whisky (which put me in the realm of the angels).

Once, when Omar had come to get some Grandpa headache powders for his ailing Bette, I asked if he'd ever been to jail.

Yes, he said.

For stealing? I probed.

"No, Mr. Gentleman Robert," he protested. "I'm not a thief."

"For what, then? Murder?"

He nodded with a grin.

"How many people have you killed?"

"Millions," he replied.

Obviously I laughed.

At which he lent towards me and whispered, in a radiating cloud of alcohol, "It was this finger"—he stuck his right claw-nailed index finger so close to my nose I went squint—"that pressed the button to drop the bomb on Hiroshima!"

Two days later, a sprightly Bette came to thank me for the medicine (and, to be honest, relieve me of a burdensome couple of rand that was clearly preventing me from entering the kingdom of heaven).

"The good lord Jesus is going to look after you," she assured me once the money had changed hands.

"I don't think he's doing a good job at the moment," I told her. (Justine had recently delivered a package that contained the shredded remains of my love letters to her. Luke, for his part, was acting exceedingly strange.)

"Are you cross with the good lord Jesus?" Bette asked with a grimace of absolute disbelief.

"Very cross," I confirmed.

She stared at me as if I was being unusually stupid.

"Ag, for shame, Mr. Gentleman," she said. "So what!"

15

To be precise it was on Thursday, 24 August 1995, that I received the third and last unanticipated package, also sent from Johannesburg, also without explanatory note. Inside the padded envelope were two large feint-ruled exercise books glued together into a single book, and a short newspaper clipping. Obviously I read this first. It was dated in pencil 22 November 1994.

Malitia: A South African tourist was murdered here last week. This is the fifth fatal attack on tourists in the last three months. Police say they have arrested two suspects.

The tourist, identified as Christo Mercer, was attacked in a busy street by muggers who stabbed him before running off with his wallet.

According to the Johannesburg travel agents, International Adventures, who organized Mr Mercer's trip, he was travelling alone. The spokesman said he was fulfilling the dream of a lifetime by journeying across the Sahara.

Mr Mercer's next-of-kin have been notified but were unavailable for comment.

I had no idea what this cutting was meant to tell me, since at the time there was no logical connection between this unfortunate tourist and the writings I had received.

At first the exercise book was likewise baffling. Though it

gave me names such as Wilma and Olive and Emily, initially they were meaningless. Only when it came to the death of the four virgins did the proverbial penny drop. But this still didn't explain the newspaper clipping, unless I was supposed to assume by some wild intuitive leap—which I did—that the writer and the dreamer and the tourist were one. And even this did not explain why I should be vaguely interested in a demented midlife drop-out who ends up dead in a place called Malitia, wherever that might be.

But at least the plot had thickened.

On the inside cover of the exercise book was the title "The Book of Dreams," and beneath it:

> *Dream a dream thrice*
> *cockatrice.*

In the library's copy of the *Longman Dictionary of the English Language* a cockatrice is described as "A mythical serpent that was hatched by a reptile from a cock's egg and that had a glance that could kill."

According to Brewer's *Concise Dictionary of Phrase and Fable* (London, 1993) it is "A fabulous and heraldic monster with the wings of a fowl, tail of a dragon, and head of a cock; the same as basilisk. Isaiah says, 'the weaned child shall put his head on the cockatrice' den' (xi, 8) to signify that the most obnoxious animal shall not hurt the most feeble of God's creatures. Figuratively, it means an insidious, treacherous person bent on mischief."

Brewer's gives a basilisk as "The fabulous king of serpents (Gr *basileus*, a king), also called a cockatrice and alleged to be hatched by a serpent from a cock's egg. It was reputed to be capable of 'looking anyone dead on whom it fixes its eyes.'"

For the rest the book was filled with 4,571 dreams, dated from 1975 to 11 November 1994, two days before his death.

Where each dream occurred and whether it was an original or a repeat were also noted.

The first dream was the one about eating lobsters (see chapter 1), the last about being in New York, a post-apocalyptic utopian Manhattan.

"I am in New York," the latter read. "I have never been to New York but I know it is New York even though most of its famous buildings are missing. There is no rubble or signs of disaster, just the empty spaces where the tall buildings used to be. No one seems bothered by these gaps. There is no traffic. Everyone is very happy. They are laughing and singing all the time. I walk along the pavements which are fairly busy and the vendors cooking food hand me baked potatoes or sausages as I pass. There are tourists looking at the vacant place where the Empire State Building once stood. A street artist is painting the building as if it were a small flower before her. She is a radiation victim. She has only got one eye."

So what? What exactly is that supposed to tell anyone?

Or this: "There are bodies everywhere and fires and cattle wandering about. A village burns. I am with a group of men walking slowly among the dead. We are led by two missionaries. It is sunset. Sometimes dying men rise up and try to attack us but we shoot them and they are flung down. We collect things from the dead and place them in a bag which is strung from the saddle of a horse. I don't know what these things are."

For the most part Christo Mercer's dreams display extreme paranoia and anxiety. But then, that seems to be the nature of dreams anyhow. Many of his, though, are about death. A lot are about such mundane items as onions. Actually, the book's a nightmare, a surrealistic vision of horror. If I were the dreamer I'd be locked away in a cell with padded walls. Surely no sane human being can face this kind of kaleidoscope at night and still behave rationally during the day.

What, for instance, would Freud or Jung make of this? "I am running down a path and I have a feeling that Wilma is with me and we have to get to this house that we can see at the end. On one side of the path is a fence and on the other a hedge. The hedge has grown over the path so that it forms a tunnel. The next thing we are walking down the Strand or Oxford Street. Wilma wants to stay up all night but I want to go to this B&B that's just £10 a night. We get to the house and it's the house that was at the end of the path. In our room there are four deformed baby girls lying on the bed. They are dead."

I have no idea why Christo Mercer had this obsession with his dreams. He derided therapists, and as far as I can ascertain he didn't view the dreams in either Freudian or Jungian terms as pathways to greater truths.

Freud, from what I gathered by flipping through some reference books (this time I've decided to stay clear of professors), described dreams as "a disguised fulfillment of repressed wishes." Generally these "repressed wishes" had occurred in the past twenty-four hours; and by a process of "free association," the dreamer could uncover his complexes. So I suppose you could say that the lobster-eating dream signifies the complete demolition of Jorge Morate and his absorption into the life of Christo Mercer.

You can take this one step further by referring to that handy little undergraduate book, *What Freud Really Said*, in which David Stafford-Clarke interprets Freud's observations on the angst in our dreams as follows: "Anxiety in dreams is often aroused even by the disguised fulfillment of a repressed wish [the lobster meal as symbolic of the Christian resurrection myth!], particularly if the original repression was necessary to spare the patient anguish, guilt, or apprehension.

"From the psychological standpoint, however, the function of the dream is to discharge the tensions of the repressed and forbidden wish [Christo Mercer's guilt at Morate's death, not to mention the four virgins]. If these are extreme, the dream will be charged with anxiety, and indeed the process may be unsuccessful and the sleeper may wake, probably feeling and displaying the signs of anxiety and disturbance [witness his apprehension and weird behaviour after the dream recurred] appropriate to the threatening but repressed emotion."

Certainly having a face stare up at you from among the shattered remains of the lobster you've just consumed and tell you you've been poisoned is going to lead to great feelings of anxiety. At least for me it would. Then I, too, would want to smash up the world like Tamburlaine.

If, on the other hand, we took the Jungian perspective and dispensed with the "free association" lark, we'd regard the lobster not as symbolic of a frustrated sexuality (a long, hard penile-like creature that penetrates into dark rocky crevices for its food) but as a lobster, and probably would tap into the "collective unconscious." For Jung it's important that Christo Mercer's unconscious chose a lobster (probably from the west coast, *Jasus lalandii*) and not, say, a Sri Lankan cane rat to dine on. What this actually tells us about Christo Mercer, I can't say. I'm no dream merchant, myself.

But consider the lobster as archetype. Whereas Freud considered archetypes as "archaic remnants" left over from earlier stages of our evolution, merely attached to our minds in much the way an appendix is attached to the intestine, for Jung archetypes grant us meaning and religious significance.

In that truly fascinating book *Man and His Symbols*, which has been distracting me for the last two days, Jung says, "the psychologist must have a sufficient experience not only of dreams and other products of unconscious activity, but also of mythology in its widest sense. Without this equipment, nobody can spot the important analogies: it is not possible, for instance, to see the analogy between a case of compulsion neurosis and that of a classical demonic possession without a working knowledge of both." On the basis of my albeit limited reading, I'd say that's exactly what we're dealing with here.

In other words, if I understand Jung correctly (not an easy thing to do), Christo Mercer's lobster was going beyond the merely personal into the mythic. This is deep water indeed. Murky stuff. What we're talking about here is what lurks in the darkness of the human soul. In all of us. It's what you could call the experience of humanity, to coin a phrase.

And having gone this far, let's venture further and see the lobster, or the virgins, or the bombed version of New York, or the house of dead babies, or the onions, or the cuttlefish (see chapter 32) as a "manifestation of the psyche"—a phrase much beloved by psychologists. In layman's terms this means we're dreaming continuously and, moreover, that we're not only the dreamers but the subjects of our dreams. Or, put another way, we're experiencing our myths as real happenings in our lives. This, perhaps, is the clue to reading Christo Mercer's story.

And after witnessing the transformation of Justine, I'm inclined to support this theory.

16

About five days after receiving the dream-book package I returned home from a consultation with my lawyer—Justine had let me know we should start divorcing, acrimoniously—to find a raspy, hardly audible message on my answering machine. The voice sounded like Marlon Brando in *Apocalypse Now*, so I had to listen to it a number of times:

Ah, Mr. Poley, I'm pleased you're not in. How's the weather in Cape Town today? You don't know me, Mr. Poley, and there's no need for you to know me. I'm the one who sent you all the fascinating presents. But there's a lot more I can tell you about Christo Mercer. There's a lot more I'm going to tell you about him. It's in the post to you, Mr. Poley. I'm sure you will be interested. Oh, and I've taken the liberty of recommending a few hotels you might need.

That was the one and only time I ever heard—in the strictest sense of this word—from "my source." For not entirely original reasons I've called him Deep Throat II.

True to his word, a remarkably detailed file giving most of the salient biographical information on this mysterious stranger arrived a few days later. Of course it left a number of questions unanswered, such obvious and disturbing ones as:

1. How did Deep Throat II get his hands on Christo Mercer's possessions, especially those from Malitia?

2. How did Deep Throat II get the biographical file?

3. Why was such a file kept in the first place?

4. Where was the file kept?

5. Why did Deep Throat II choose me?

To Question 1 I now have an answer, of sorts (see chapter 32). Question 2 conjures up totally sinister dealings. There will never be an answer to either this or Questions 3 and 4. There will, however, remain the hints of state security and military intelligence and ominous, faceless figures in the background.

To me, personally, number 5 was the most alarming question of all. I should explain: my name, as you know, is Robert Poley. You probably recognize it, and might well have read at least one of my five books. At forty-three I'm a former journalist, a successful writer of what literary snobs call "airport fiction"—

the high-action low-demand escapades where the women are beautiful and dangerous or beautiful and submissive, and the men (like those machos in the Camel adverts) drive 4x4s, take their holidays in deserts or forests, shoot lions, fish for marlin, fuck whatever broads are available. They have names like Katie Crane or Brian Dermott. This sort of thing is always happening to them:

"It's me," she said softly. "Katie. I couldn't sleep. I'm dreadfully sorry I'm not a Masai maiden and couldn't find a spear to stick in front of your *manyatta,* but I've brought the shotgun and it's resting on your camp chair and I'm wearing a nightgown instead of pyjamas. Do you think that might serve to establish my intentions? The nightgown is a little wet in the hem. I hope you won't mind."

"You're quite sure?" Brian's voice came thick from the black interior of the tent. "You're quite sure." The second time was a statement.

"Quite, quite sure," she said, and felt him beside her in the blackness. She thought she heard the wet thump of his tent flaps falling before he took her in his arms. Suddenly Katie Crane did not mind that she was coming back in the rain to feed on someone else's kill.

No, this is not self-promotion. It's a quote from one of the greats of the "airport school," not Wilbur Smith but Robert Ruark. In fact it's from his seminal work on African independence, *Uhuru,* published—in London, of course—in 1962. I write this sort of stuff myself because I enjoy writing it. Professor Richard Khafulo's "Oh, dear!" is inaudible beneath the ring of cash registers. Which is the other reason for my chosen genre: it pays real money. When I hear what earnest authors are offered as advances I want to cry. I wouldn't be able to live on their earnings. More importantly, I couldn't afford to divorce Justine.

Which brings me again to the unsettling Question 5: why me? If Deep Throat II had contacted Rian Malan, that I could've understood. It's his kind of territory. But a popular writer doesn't make sense. Even so I have a theory: Deep Throat II spends (or spent) a lot of time in airports; he's read my thrillers. And he can't tell the difference between their world and his own. As for his motives, they might be anything from revenge to righteous indignation. My motives are far simpler. I'm constantly in search of plots and intrigue—and this particular one, in those despairing days of post-apartheid revelation, couldn't have rung truer. There's also something of the journalist's curiosity left in me.

And there was Justine's malevolence to be distracted from.

Just as now I need to be distracted from Luke, who wants to come and live with me. Yesterday he was sentenced to four weekends' community service at a drug rehabilitation centre named for St. Anthony, the patron saint of gravediggers, as it happens (*vide* Brewer's).

PART III

Truth

17

The life of Christopher Edward Mercer began at three o'clock in the afternoon in the Hillbrow Hospital, Johannesburg, on Sunday, 12 September 1954. His mother, Florence, was twenty-nine years old; his father, Jack, twenty-eight. Christo was their firstborn, and baptized, in October, in the city's Central Methodist Church. Three years later his sister, Mary, was born in the same hospital. For the next two decades Christo Mercer lived in the suburb of Linden.

His father, a life insurance salesman for Liberty & Federal, earned enough money to run an Austin A40 and take the family on an annual holiday to the Natal coast. His mother's job was to raise the children.

Christo Mercer attended first the Risidale Primary School and then Roosevelt Park High School. In 1971, his final year, he was a prefect. He received colours for rugby, cricket, and athletics. He won the school's English short story competition. He matriculated with a distinction in English and impressive pass marks in Afrikaans, history, mathematics, science, and accounting.

From 1972 to 1974, he was registered for a BA at the University of the Witwatersrand, majoring in law and English. During this time he published poetry in various magazines. His keen participation in sport had by this point dwindled to nothing.

In 1975 he was conscripted into the army to undergo his national service. As a graduate he could have chosen the easy way out and become an officer, a glorified administrative clerk, and passed a safe and easy two years. He went, as he had been allocated, into 1SAI, an infantry division, knowing that he would be sent to northern Namibia (then called South West Africa and illegally administered by South Africa), where intensifying guerrilla activity by SWAPO (the South West African People's Organization) was turning the border with Angola into a war zone.

Christo Mercer's regiment was ordered to the frontier in November 1975. He was based there until the following March and then again from June to September. He was discharged in December 1976, yet even so he faced a series of three-month camps every year for at least the next decade. He was called up again in 1977 and 1978 to complete these duties. After that he did no further military service. Possibly he was considered too valuable to be wasted as cannon fodder!

It was during his stint in the army that Christo Mercer started his book of dreams. It was on the border that he befriended Martin Eloff, beginning a relationship that would last the rest of his life. Eloff was also an avid reader and a poet, although he wrote in Afrikaans.

Christo Mercer's working career begins quite ordinarily in 1976 at the law offices of Heunis, Hamman & Mostert, where he worked as an articled clerk. Of the original partners, P. J. P. Mostert is the only one alive. When he retired seven years ago, the firm changed its name to Muller & Muller, though it remains in the same suite of offices in Azalea Chambers, Paul Kruger Street, Pretoria.

How Christo Mercer came to work at Heunis, Hamman & Mostert owes nothing to favour or the old-boy network. Once discharged from the army, he responded to a placement advertisement and was hired, Mostert says, because his degree marks were impressive, he'd done his national service and "proved himself a man," and because English was his first language.

Just under eighteen months after joining the law firm he married twenty-year-old Wilma Mostert in the Pretoria Dutch Reformed Church. He was twenty-three years old. She moved into his one-bedroomed flat in Arcadia, which had a view over the central city that would fill lesser souls with despair.

But in 1977 the newlyweds had other matters to think about. Wilma was still a student at the local teachers training college, and Christo was planning to improve his qualifications. In 1978 Christo Mercer registered at the Transvaal Technikon and completed, part-time, a year-long diploma in management and administration. No one can confirm if he did this of his own accord or at the behest of his father-in-law. The suspicions are that Mostert encouraged him in this direction.

In June 1978 his father, aged fifty-two, died suddenly of a perforated bowel. The following year, Christo Mercer joined Precision Engineering. Quite why he made a career change from legal matters to business is unclear. Given the nature of his position at Precision Engineering, it's tempting to think that his diploma in business administration might have had something to do with it. But it's rather more likely that his father-in-law was a greater factor. (On this Mostert refuses comment.)

According to the register of companies, Precision Engineering was a private company that began operating out of premises on Main Reef Road, Denver, an industrial complex east of downtown Johannesburg, on 23 November 1979. Four directors are listed: M. T. Cronje, A. Kirkland, P. J. P. Mostert, and D. M. Walton (British). While employed by Precision Engineering, Christo Mercer completed an MBA at the University of Cape Town. For the whole of 1984 he and his wife lived in Cape Town. Early in the year—9 March—their first daughter, Olive, was born; but Christo Mercer didn't seem to find the baby an interruption to his studies. He completed the course with his customary ability and won the Old Mutual gold medal for academic excellence.

In September 1985, Precision Engineering was suddenly closed down. Christo Mercer probably didn't lose any sleep over this, stepping as he did straight into the offices of International Ventures.

Once again according to the register of companies: International Ventures was registered in October 1985 and listed a street address of 212 Beatrix Street, Arcadia, Pretoria. No such number has ever existed in Beatrix Street. The postal box number, however, is correct and has remained the same for ten years. There were two directors in 1985: Philip Kleinsmidt and Christo Mercer. In 1988 one John Campbell became another. Four years later his name was deleted from the register.

In 1986 Christo Mercer began his visits to northern Africa, and met the warlord Ibn el-Tamaru at his stronghold in Djano. Thereafter, if his travel schedule is anything to go by, business picked up significantly. His sister, Mary Fitzgerald, believes he was travelling out of the country between ten and fifteen times a year.

At home, too, things were blossoming. A second daughter, Emily, was born on 22 July 1988. The family had started taking holidays in Mauritius. In 1989 he bought two new BMWs, and three years later traded them both against new 5- and 3-series models.

By now Christo Mercer was a seasoned sojourner among his clients in the north. He had opened an office of International Ventures in a rented house in Malitia in June 1993 and employed a full-time manager, Oumou Sangaré, and various domestic staff supplied to him by Ibn el-Tamaru. International Ventures, thanks to Christo Mercer, had moved into a lucrative market.

In the greater scheme of things they were small-timers; but to the warlords of the Sahel, the appearance of this long, mournful face was not an insignificant event. And the sight of him perching awkwardly on their cushions was truly reassuring.

Today the Pretoria street address of International Ventures is on the appropriately named Bloed Street, around the corner from the National Zoological Gardens. The house, converted into office premises, is protected by high walls and razor wire and security doors.

The company is under a judicial investigation into the arms trade.

Note 1: Photographs of the young Christo Mercer show a boy who seldom smiles. Two family snaps in particular foretell his life. In the first he sits reading in a deck chair, his legs swinging clear of the sand. In the second he's wearing cowboy leggings and a shirt with fringed sleeves, a wide-brimmed hat, and a belt with two holsters. As he points a cap gun at the camera, his eyes are hidden behind a Zorro-like mask, a bandit's bandanna covering his nose and mouth. His pose is so formal that he looks awkward.

Note 2: As a sullen adolescent in the suburb of Linden, Christo Mercer probably went to what were then called "sessions"— today's teenagers know them as techno raves—at the Lemon Squeezer, a hall shaped like its name in the grounds of a local Catholic church. Here he would've faced the temptations of liquor and dagga, and most probably succumbed to their heady experiences. Here he may have had prolonged embraces with various girlfriends, tried to squeeze their Maidenform-ed breasts, kissed them for so long that he would undoubtedly have suffered the uncomfortable condition known as "lover's balls."

Note 3: In 1974, the tense situation on the Namibian border was exacerbated by the coup d'état in Portugal, which ushered in the decolonization of the Portuguese empire in Africa. By the end of 1975 Angola and Mozambique were independent, though civil war broke out in Angola almost immediately. South Africa promptly invaded the country, ostensibly at the behest of Zambia and Zaire and with the initial cooperation of the United States. Cuba came to the support of the Angolan government, and the South African forces were stopped and made to retreat.

Note 4: When Christo Mercer joined Heunis, Hamman & Mostert, the firm was fiercely Afrikaans—Hamman apparently could not and would not speak English—though willing, apparently, to allow this "Englishman" to help them extend their business in the future.

"Buitendien," according to Mrs. Magda Mostert (soon to be his mother-in-law) on behalf of her husband, "hy het so 'n opregte jong man gelyk." And so this sincere and frank young man was given a position as a legal clerk.

From having spent months dealing in death and destruction, Christo Mercer suddenly found himself doing legal research and drafting rudimentary documents in a quiet office five floors above the streets. He would have looked out at the windows of another office block.

Note 5: Mostert won't talk about what sort of work his firm handled in the seventies. However, three clippings in the morgue at the *Pretoria News* (dated 11–13 June 1973) give a few details about the divorce proceedings of M. T. Cronje *vs.* B. J. Cronje—a case reported probably because the former Cronje was a member of parliament and the latter a great-granddaughter of the Boer War hero General De la Rey. The lawyer representing M. T. Cronje was none other than P. J. P. Mostert.

Mostert's involvement with the Cronje case also seems to suggest that he had access to well-positioned people in government, and so perhaps he was the initiator of Christo Mercer's subsequent career in the arms industry.

Note 6: In Christo Mercer's book of dreams is this entry dated 14 June 1978 (four days after his father's death): "I am sitting on a stoep reading. I don't know what the book is. The stoep is in shadow but beyond it there is such bright sunlight I cannot see anything. But it feels like the Karoo. I look up from the book and the shadows turn into elephants that move off into the light. I am terribly afraid."

Note 7: Christo Mercer's MBA degree was almost certainly underwritten by the company. This, at any rate, is often how these degrees are financed. That Precision Engineering, then just four years old, could send their production manager away for a year on a highly expensive course indicates that the company was operating efficiently and making money. Or maybe these criteria weren't important, if a larger institution (like the state) was doing the bankrolling.

Note 8: For his MBA technical report—an obligatory thesis— Christo Mercer analyzed the effect of sanctions as a moral and practical form of censuring a wayward government. Informative but dull, it documents Stalin leaning on Yugoslavia in the 1920s, the British response to Mussolini's invasion of Abyssinia in 1935, the Anglo-American measures which led to the reinstatement of the Shah in Iran in 1953, and, of course, the sanctions instituted against Rhodesia from 1965.

In his concluding remarks he writes: "A siege psychosis once engendered can be a powerful factor in sustaining the will to resist, as well as a useful support for a government intent on applying such unpopular measures as tax increases. The more cohesive a society is the more likely [it is] a government will be able to draw on previously dormant or unsuspected reserves of strength." He then quotes the case of increased production in Italy in the late thirties, and in Rhodesia in the ten years up to 1975. At the time, 1984, sanctions against South Africa were becoming tougher.

Note 9: Of the directors at Precision Engineering, what is known is that Walton ran an engineering company called Omega Engineering in Coventry, UK; Cronje of the famous divorce was Minister of Trade and Industry in the first P. W. Botha cabinet; and Kirkland, a former rugby player, was a general in the South African Defence Force. A month after the company was closed in September 1985, the *Star* carried an advertisement which listed office furniture and various die-cutting and tooling machines from Precision Engineering being placed on auction.

Neither Mostert nor Kirkland will talk about what Precision Engineering produced. (In 1983 Cronje suffered a stroke which left him paralyzed and in need of constant medical supervision. He cannot talk or do anything for himself.) Walton, however, was arrested in October 1985 in Britain, and appeared in court six months later on charges of breaking the arms embargo against South Africa.

His company manufactured under licence an air-to-air missile called a V3B. The court ruled that Walton was responsible for selling design plans of the missile as well as tooling equipment for its manufacture to Precision Engineering. V3Bs were mounted on the Mirage III and F-1 fighters. According to experts they are short-range, dogfight missiles, and their main advantage is that their seekerhead can find targets not directly in front of the aircraft. They were used by the South African Air Force in the final phase of the intervention in the Angolan civil war (1987–88).

Walton was found guilty as charged and sentenced to five years' imprisonment. He died shortly after his release in 1990. The cause of his death is unknown.

Note 10: International Ventures belongs to that rash of mysterious companies set up by exposed spies and apparently retired security policemen in the mid to late eighties: operations—like those started by spymaster Craig Williamson—purporting to offer industrial security services.

Unlike Williamson's concerns, though, International Ventures received no media coverage until it was linked, in January 1993, to mercenary activity in Angola. But even that story soon ran out of substance; the company's only comment, attributed to director Philip Kleinsmidt, was that they acted as transport carriers for North American and European aid agencies.

Even the killing of Christo Mercer occasioned only two mentions in daily newspapers, one of which I've already quoted. The Sundays and television ignored the incident. Radio 702 carried a cryptic item, as did the English service of the national station, the SABC. And then both Christo Mercer and International Ventures dropped out of the public mind until 17 September 1995, when an article on South Africa's arms trade in the *Sunday Times* mentioned his name in passing.

Note 11: Craig Williamson was a security police spy who infiltrated and disrupted the activities of the South Africa Communist Party. A security force member for seventeen years, he was much decorated for his duplicity. He has subsequently been linked with hit-squad activities, and implicated in the 1982 bombing of ANC House in Islington, London.

After resigning in 1985, Williamson began infiltrating the upper echelons of industry, commerce, and government as a director of companies and also was nominated a National Party member of the President's Council. During the late eighties he was chiefly involved in negotiating takeover deals between European multinationals and companies divesting their South African interests.

The engorged spider and its web is not an inappropriate metaphor here.

Note 12: Readers may see some similarities between Craig Williamson and my hirsute, rotund spy, Crag Wilson, who was forever spilling food on his clothes. However, I want to state unequivocally that the obese hero of my 1991 best-seller, *Who Lurks in the Shadows,* is wholly fictional.

Note 13: Christo Mercer's material situation improved hugely during his time with International Ventures. As noted, in early 1986 he moved into the large house—his English "cottage"—in Waterkloof. Previously he had rented an unpretentious home in the Johannesburg suburb of Parktown North, where the family stayed while he worked for Precision Engineering.

Note 14: John Campbell, the third director of International Ventures, is ("was" may already be appropriate) a known mercenary, and has been involved in African revolutions since the Belgian Congo insurrection in the early sixties. His last known escapade was the abortive Seychelles coup led by Colonel Mad Mike Hoare in 1981. Campbell, along with his commander, was sentenced to ten years' imprisonment by a South African court. However, after serving little more than two years, then State President P. W. Botha pardoned them.

III

Note 15: There is a Wassoulou singer called Oumou Sangaré. Both that Oumou Sangaré and Christo Mercer's Oumou Sangaré have voices to melt the heart. But the latter is not the former.

Note 16: Obviously Philip Kleinsmidt won't admit that International Ventures is trading in illegal arms, despite the mass of information to the contrary. However, as I've stated, the company is being investigated as part of a judicial inquiry into Armscor, the state weapons agency.

Armscor was South Africa's response to the United Nations arms embargo, instituted in 1963. By the early eighties, Armscor "controlled subsidiaries which built military aircraft, firearms, and artillery pieces of very high quality, as well as missile-guidance and radar systems, and various types of military vehicle adapted . . . for conflict under local conditions. . . . Arms production was based on the possession of a steel industry in which a plentiful supply of all the strategic minerals was married to expert technology, initially imported, and subsequently trained on the spot. By 1983 South Africa was producing weapons for export"—T. R. H. Davenport, *South Africa: A Modern History* (Johannesburg: Macmillan South Africa, 1987).

By 1992, two shiploads of Armscor weaponry—mines, mortar rounds, hundreds of thousands of rounds of rifle and shotgun ammunition—were reported to have ended up in Croatia, in contravention of another UN arms embargo.

In 1995, Denel, an arms manufacturer within the Armscor umbrella, exported weaponry to seventy countries for a return of $330 million. This included missiles to Pakistan, G5 cannons to the Persian Gulf, Rooivalk attack helicopters to Malaysia. Despite this, in the 1995/1996 annual report, Denel's chairman, D. C. Brink, states: "Over the review period neither Denel nor the regulating bodies have been sufficiently adept at 'weaving the desired tapestry' to ensure success in available and lucrative markets."

Note 17: "Weaving the desired tapestry" is such a poetic gloss for "placing enough arms dealers with enough weapons of death in the field" that I had to find its source. So I faxed Eben Mouton at Denel's Communications Department: "Dear Mr. Mouton, I am an English teacher and use annual reports as teaching aids. In Denel's latest report there is a phrase in the eighth paragraph within quotation marks: 'weaving the desired tapestry.' I assume this is a literary quotation but have been unable to source it and would be most grateful if you could give me the reference."

When, after ten days, there had been no response I telephoned his office. His secretary giggled and promised to answer my fax. Nothing, however, was forthcoming. "Weaving the desired tapestry" has the sort of flourish Christo Mercer might have used in his poetry. Perhaps the industry attracts these sensitive souls!

18

On Saturday, 30 September 1995, I flew to Johannesburg to start my investigations into the life and times of Christo Mercer

I was glad to be leaving Cape Town for a few days. In addition to my notes and tape recorder I had a letter from Justine's lawyers in my shoulder bag. She was demanding house, both cars, furniture, my books, my desk, my imitation flintlock pistols, my ship in a bottle—everything, in a word, including a percentage of any future royalties earned from books I'd written while we were married.

Alarmed, I spoke to my lawyer, who didn't sound as reassuring as a man in this situation would've liked. The bitch, I thought. The bitch.

And then there was Luke. He'd come straight from school to Victoria Court the previous afternoon, reiterating his desire to live with me.

"But you can't, Luke," I said, while the sadness behind his words settled in my chest with a heaviness that I knew would take a long time to disperse. And I couldn't look at his face when I told him this.

He didn't have to say, Why not? The *why* screamed at me from where he sat slouched in my one and only easy chair, staring at his shoes. His hair was cut so short he was almost a skinhead. He now had five earrings. At the trial there'd been only the one.

"You can't, Luke," I said again. "Look at this place. It's all right for me, but you need a home. You need someone to cook your meals and do your washing and make sure you get up on time. You need space, Luke. You need a room of your own. You need to be near school. You need to be near your friends. You need Matthew. Probably he needs you, I don't know. And what about your mother? Have you thought about her? You're her son, Luke; you can't just walk out on her."

He was crying. He was trying not to let me see, but he was crying. I could hear it in his breathing. I was desperate.

"Jesus, Luke. I'd have you here this minute if I had the right place. But I don't. You can't sleep on the floor."

"You could get somewhere," he said.

"I can't just get somewhere, Luke. For Christ's sake, do you think this is easy for me? Your mother's gone mad. I've got the police telling me you're a drug addict. I don't need this, Luke. I can't cope with all this."

I must admit we were both in tears now. I didn't know what to do. The whole world was suddenly new to me. And terrifying.

Then he said, "Mom told me this is what you'd say."

I can imagine what it's like to be hit unexpectedly in the face by someone wielding a cricket bat. The stunning blackness. The crash against the bone beating out all other sound. The heat and the pain, pain that takes you down to the floor. "What?" I whispered, fighting for breath. "She said *what*?"

I couldn't look at him. I didn't want to. "Fuck it, Luke! What're you doing to me?"

He said nothing.

Eventually I was able to stand up again. I walked around, try-ing to get my breathing back to normal, trying to think straight.

Why can't you have him with you? He's your son, for Christ's sake. He's fucked up because he doesn't know what's going on. His world's shattered. So's yours, but you're his father. Help him. But I couldn't, not yet. I had to find my way first.

"Okay," I said at last. "Okay. I'll find another place. But you're going to have to wait, Luke. I can't do it now. Next year, probably."

I don't know how it went from there. . . . No, I do know, but I'm not about to tell it. Sometimes the pain will allow only so much truth.

Thank God I was able to fly off somewhere else. Thank God I had my investigations, my Christo Mercer.

19

In my preliminary inquiries Wilma Mercer had refused to be interviewed or to answer queries by letter. I never even got to speak with her on the telephone. I was referred by her father to her lawyer, Jan Muller, who agreed to see me. This is the entire content of our tape-recorded interview:

"Mr. Poley, I'm sorry you've had to come all this way, but I felt it was important that I stress to you in person that Mrs.

Mercer is under no circumstances to be harassed. She does not want to see you or answer any questions. She would like you to drop this whole project, although she realizes she has no legal means of preventing what she sees as a gross invasion of her own and of her daughters' privacy. I should also like to make it clear that should you try to get in touch with her in any way, or try to talk to Olive or Emily, I shall apply for a court interdict restraining you. I'm sorry if this sounds unnecessarily threatening, but my client particularly wanted you to know how opposed she is to your project. I hope you will respect her privacy and that we won't have to take matters any further."

"There is a judicial—"

"I'm sorry, I'm not prepared to say anything more on this matter. Ek het klaar gepraat, Meneer Poley."

(Personal interview: Pretoria; Monday, 2 October 1995)

Note: The Afrikaans phrase is both a threat and a warning, perhaps best translated as: "That's all, Mr. Poley." When used aggressively the honorific "meneer" carries more than a hint of sarcasm.

20

The Mosterts live in one of those new walled enclaves for the monied aged which are becoming so popular on the outskirts of our bigger cities. For a considerable investment you can retire to a home in a complex of neat lawns and trimmed edges that boasts twenty-four-hour security, a Gary Player–designed golf course, a frail care centre, library, pubs, lounges—everything those in their twilight years might desire. These fortified havens of peace and tranquillity are named Ibis Valley, or Morgenster, or Clé du Cap. Or, like the Mosterts' very own,

Magersfontein. I interviewed P. J. P. (Paul) Mostert on the stoep of his condo.

My friend, I'm an old man. There are things I don't get upset about anymore. If I see a lone cockroach scuttle across the floor, I don't go searching for it with the can of Doom. If I see a fly has settled on the food, I don't even brush it away. What does it matter if we eat a speck of flydirt. In eighty years one speck of flydirt, ten specks of flydirt, it doesn't mean anything.

And this is why I said I would talk to you. Whatever kak you are going to bring into my life doesn't matter. Maybe it never mattered. Maybe we should just have brushed you muckrakers away as if you were flies.

But twenty years ago, forty years ago, fifty years ago, then I wouldn't have let you put your foot inside my door. Just as then I would have squashed the cockroaches and swatted the flies, so I would have taken a sjambok to your hide. I could have whipped every reporter, every writer, without a moment's mercy. Especially you English. There were times at the political meetings in the fifties when I did.

There are scum on this earth, my friend, but there is none worse than your sort. There never has been worse and there never will be worse. And you know why, because you tell bloody lies, that's why. The truth is never good enough for you.

You come here and you say you're writing about Christo because you think he's a hero. As you put it, an unsung hero. Ja, my friend, that is what I say. It is what the dominee said at the funeral. Maybe you will even write what I have said in your book. But I know you are lying. I have seen so many people lie that I know you are lying.

You don't think Christo was a hero, do you, my friend? I don't know what you think he was and I don't care. You said on the phone you wanted to know what I thought about this business; well, I'm going to tell you. But what I tell you you won't have the guts to publish. Because you, my friend, will see the truth is too tough for you.

You want to know who killed him? I'll tell you: Mossad agents. You want to know why! Go and ask the Israelis. You want to know how I know. It's because I have been told. I still have friends where it counts.

Maybe you saw in the newspaper the other day there was a short piece—I cut it out—about some major in military intelligence who was found stabbed in the throat with a stiletto blade. She and her husband. It was Mossad. The police know it was Mossad. The government knows it was Mossad. The Jews know it was Mossad.

The Mossad people have no compunction. They'll kill for what is no reason at all. You go and ask the police. They've got records of how many people Mossad have killed here: scientists, military, diplomats. On the record they'll tell you all those killings were just unlucky: victims of violent robbery. Off the record they'll tell you it's Mossad.

But what can they do? Nothing. And why? Because it's too complicated. It's trade-offs and big money and it goes right to the top. It's dirty, my friend, very dirty. You've got to be brave or very stupid to play with things like this. Which is why I say the truth is too tough for you and your book. You want to live like that Muslim writer, what's his name . . . Rushdie?

Let me tell you something, my friend, something you're going to think is cold-hearted, but that won't stop it from being true. You see, my friend, every night I thank God they didn't do it when Christo was at home. They'd have killed them all. Wilma, the girls, all of them.

It's not a nice thing to say, I know, but I'm a man who's not afraid of speaking his mind. And so I say thank God that it didn't happen here. It's a pity it had to happen at all, but a man in that business knows the sort of risks he runs; Christo knew that.

And he knew about Jews. For years he's been—how do you English say—thick as thieves with the Israelis. I didn't like it. I told him, You watch your back, my boy. Maybe they gave us atomic know-how, maybe we helped them explode their bombs, but the Jews are only friends with you while you've got something they want and the price is right. When that changes you can forget it. You're as good as dead. I've seen it over and over again. I've seen it in business. I've seen it in politics. I've seen it when Christians try to marry Jewish women. It doesn't work, my friend; it's like whites marrying blacks: it doesn't work.

(Personal interview: Pretoria; Monday, 2 October 1995)

Note 1: Magersfontein was the site of a famous Boer victory during the Anglo-Boer War. Albeit at a cost to themselves of 236 dead, the Boers inflicted a body count of 902 among the British forces. Most of the Tommies were shot in the back as they tried to flee from the trap into which their officers had marched them. For a detailed description of the slaughter, see pages 201–06 of Thomas Pakenham's *The Boer War* (London: Weidenfeld and Nicolson, 1979).

Note 2: The military victim Mostert referred to is Major Juanita du Plessis, who with her husband, André, was murdered on 3 August 1995 (see the *Mail & Guardian*, 8 September 1995).

Note 3: "[By 1983] cooperation with Israel and Taiwan in the design and manufacture of weapons was evidently close" (Davenport in his aforementioned *South Africa: A Modern History*).

Note 4: For the duration of the interview Mostert sat on a blow-up rubber ring. I suspect he has haemorrhoids and that even a thrombosis might have occurred. This, according to the *Reader's Digest Illustrated Medical Encyclopedia*, usually requires surgical removal.

21

"Come into the kitchen, Meneer Poley, and I'll make you a nice cup of coffee," said Magda Mostert, suddenly appearing when my interview with her husband was over. I stood up.

You can talk here, P. J. P. Mostert said in Afrikaans.

"You won't give me a chance to say anything," his wife replied, laughing.

Her husband glared at her. "Maak soos jy wil," he grumbled.

In the kitchen I sat down at a small breakfast bar. While she spooned some truly disgusting instant coffee into a cup—will the espresso empire never colonize Pretoria?—she told me not to be offended, that her husband didn't mean half the things he said, and that he was actually in a lot of pain. She poured boiling water onto the coffee powder and set the muck before me, spilling some in the saucer. Then, without any prompting, she began talking in Afrikaans.

It's tragic, Meneer Poley. Ai, but it makes my heart sore to think about it. He was such a lovely man.

The first time I saw him I said to myself, now here's an honest, sincere young man. I was so glad when Wilma decided to marry him. They made such a handsome bride and groom.

I don't know, Meneer Poley, but sometimes I think the world is truly an evil place. How can one man do this sort of thing to another man? It's the Arabs. You must have seen that film about the Englishman who went and lived with the Arabs. What do you say it's called? *Lawrence of Arabia*. Ja, that's it, *Lawrence of Arabia*. They're such barbarians. Such cruel people.

But still I can't understand it. I get terribly heartsore. And for the children. What are they going to do now? Their pa is dead. They loved him so much. On the weekends they used to follow him around like puppy dogs. And he always had time for them. These days most fathers are too busy to say boo or baa to their children. But not Christo. He always had time to listen to them.

When Olive started having problems with maths and science or what have you—you know they have to study such difficult subjects so young these days—it was Christo who helped her through. He had lots of patience. I can remember one Sunday afternoon how he and Olive struggled with her homework, but not for one moment did he get impatient with her. He was so gentle. And when she started to cry with frustration, he calmed her and encouraged her until she got it right. Now, you tell me how many fathers will do that? He was patient and loving with his children from the moment they were born.

He was there in the delivery ward for both births. He told me that they were the most wonderful moments of his life. I remember he said to me when Emily was born that he felt so humble watching this little life coming into the world. That's the sort of man he was, Meneer Poley. A caring, honourable man.

My Wilma couldn't have married a better man. He was a hero, just like you said. And now these blacks in the new government say he's a monster who did all sorts of horrible things. It's nonsense [she used the more expressive word: twak]. Absolute twak.

Christo was a God-fearing man. He went to church every Sunday. He thought deeply about all sorts of things. And he wouldn't open his mouth until he'd thought about what he was going to say. He was an intelligent man, Meneer Poley. He was always reading. Wilma will tell you he was an expert in old plays. He could've taught classes at the university in that subject. And now there are all these allegations and what-have-you about him. It's pure twak. Just people stirring up trouble.

Well, let me tell you I don't pay attention to their lies. I knew Christo and I know he wasn't what they said about him in the Sunday newspaper. Christo worked for the good of his country. That's the sort of man he was.

I just don't know what my Wilma is going to do now. Her life is torn to shreds. She's got to take pills. Christo died almost a year ago and still she's not coming right. I don't know. I don't know. It's tragic. I don't know what she's going to do. Heaven help us, Meneer Poley. It's a dreadful time.

(Personal interview: Pretoria; Monday, 2 October 1995)

Note: In translating my interview with Magda Mostert, I have retained the Afrikaans honorific because, in this instance, it is filled with connotations of respect and dignity.

22

Almost twenty years ago, as a young reporter, I lived in Johannesburg and worked on the *Star.* I thought then, and nothing since has changed my mind, that it was a city of hairy-backed fortune hunters. The streets smell of gold and money, when they don't reek of diesel fumes. There are men walking these pavements who will stick a gun in your ribs for whatever small change you carry; they did it a hundred years ago when the first tin shacks were built, and they're doing it still. For all that, though, Johannesburg can thrill the blood. And when the summer storms crack and sizzle across the sky, plunging forks of lightning towards the skyscrapers, I stand in awe.

One of those storms banged and rattled through the small hours before I visited Mary Fitzgerald. As I drove along the

Concrete Highway and then into the suburbs—those leafy, lush, lawned suburbs that have turned their backs on the mining camp behind the ridge—all I could smell was the damp, ripe earth. This even brought back memories of a kinder, juster Justine. God almighty, what a bitch!

However.

I drove to Mary Fitzgerald's house in Bryanston with the windows down so that the fragrance of the roadside khakibos filled the car. On the radio the jock played a straight foursome without any spots: "House of the Rising Sun," "A Whiter Shade of Pale," "Dock of the Bay," "Hotel California." This was almost paradise. I was singing. An onlooker would have said I was happy.

However.

Mary Fitzgerald is a woman of jewellery, on her body and her clothes: chains, pendants, bracelets, bangles, rings, earrings. When Mary moves, she clinks and chimes.

We sat in her white lounge to talk.

Tell me, do you pronounce your name Poley, or Pooley? Pooley. But it's only spelt with one "o." How very strange. I would've thought it was Pole-ey. It just goes to show even when it's your own language, it's easy to get it wrong. So how we're supposed to manage with these newfangled names, I don't know. Skweyiya, Kgositsile, Sibusiso. It's a nightmare. An absolute nightmare.

Christo started getting very good at clicking away with our new lords and masters, even when they were still, as he used to call them, the president's guests. Zulu's the one with the clicks, isn't it? Xhosa? No, I don't think it was Xhosa he was learning. It must've been Zulu. Maybe he just made the click sounds to impress me.

I know he was learning Zulu because they were doing some sort of training programme for the KwaZulu police. But don't ask me what. Long ago I decided I didn't want to know anything about what he was up to. And it seems to me it's just as well.

I'd better tell you my husband didn't want me to see you, and I even had that old dutchman Mostert trying to persuade me against it. But I told them both that Christo was my brother and I'm certainly not going to tell you anything I don't want to.

I'll tell you straight out I didn't like what Christo did. When I began to realize he was up to something strange . . . when was it? I don't know, exactly. Maybe four or five years ago. *When* isn't all that important. It's the *what* of it that gets to me. Anyhow, I did begin to wonder, given all that flying to north Africa. I suspected it was guns, I don't know why. Perhaps it was that guy Walton in the UK, and it doesn't really matter, but I told him straight out: Christo, if it's guns, it's not only illegal but morally wrong. I only mentioned this once and he didn't say anything, which made me think I was right.

What I'm telling you now is the only criticism I've got of Christo, and he knew it. At the end of the day it was his life and he had to live it, though whatever it was he did didn't stop me from calling him my brother. I still liked him. I still thought he was a great guy. It's just that we differed politically.

I'm not saying he was anti-Mandela or anything like that. Certainly he didn't get worked up over the inauguration like I did. I thought it was great, I cried when Mr. Mandela made his speech, but Christo was quite accepting of the election results; I suppose he voted for the Nationalists, which would've had Dad climbing up the wall in anger. And he certainly wouldn't have voted for the Democratic Party; he couldn't stand what he called "wishy-washy liberalism," which was where we had to agree to differ.

I gather you've seen the dutchman. Ma and Dad, Dad especially, couldn't understand what Christo was doing marrying an Afrikaner.

Dad was still fighting the Boer War. He'd got this personal grudge, you see. Even though he wasn't born till twenty-four years later, there was something in his blood that used to get stirred up at the mention of Afrikaners. I'm not quite sure of the story anymore, although I should be because Dad used to tell us often enough, but I think at the time his grandfather was the manager of a bank in Ficksburg. Ficksburg, I ask you! Where's Ficksburg? Who in the world knows or cares where Ficksburg is? It's somewhere in the Free State, isn't it?

Well, great-grandfather Mercer was shot up in his bank by a bunch of Boers who'd come to rob it so they'd have money to buy guns. I suppose it was the Germans running guns to them at the time. And like my brother, Christo, I'm sure the arms dealers weren't in it for the fun. Anyhow. Great-grandfather Mercer died on the wooden floor of his bank, leaving a wife pregnant with my soon-to-be-born grandfather. Hence the longstanding anti towards the dutchman. I suppose there's a sort of irony in all this, isn't there?

Anyhow. Then along comes Christo and the first thing he does is choose a Boer wife, and not just any Boer but the daughter of a Broederbonder. You didn't know that? Go look in *Superafrikaners*, you'll find Mostert listed along with the rest of the Ku Klux Klan.

You know whom he's big mates with, or was, warmonger Magnus [Malan]. How's that for a friend? Oh, he's got dirt on his hands has papa Mostert; he's a racist and an anti-Semite like you can't believe. He doesn't think Hitler gassed any Jews. He thinks the Holocaust's a Jewish invention. You'll probably find his family all belonged to the Ossewabrandwag and used to blow up railway bridges in the platteland when everyone else was at Tobruk fighting the Krauts. That's the sort of family my brother Christo marries into.

Heavens, he could be perverse sometimes. No, not sometimes. All the time. So you may well ask why'd he name the kids Olive and Emily! If Dad had been alive he'd have blown a fuse. God, that would've been the end. With Ma these things didn't matter so much and she probably wouldn't have thought about it anyhow.

I know I'm talking as if she's dead, and for the life of me there're times I look at her and I don't think she's my mother anymore. Of course she still looks like my mother, but her mind's gone. She can be absolutely lucid one moment and not there the next, as if there's been a short circuit. Pow, the wide blue yonder. But that's another story. Which neither Christo nor I could handle. Nor could Wilma, for that matter. It was her decision as much as anyone's to send Ma to Port Elizabeth. But that's long been done and there's no point in crying over it now.

Just to get back to Olive and Emily for a moment. You realize where the names come from, of course: Olive Schreiner and Emily Hobhouse. Olive, I could understand; Christo was mad about English literature—novels and poetry, too—before he got into that business of just reading Elizabethan plays.

He used to rave about *The Story of an African Farm*, so when Olive came along I didn't think too much of it. Sure, the name's a bit old-fashioned, but I've heard parents call their children worse. But with little Emily I said, Jesus, Christo, what do you think you're doing? What sort of name is Emily? And he said, It's after Emily Hobhouse. For crying out loud, I said, who cares whom it's after, it's just such an old name. You're not going to give her a chance calling her that.

But he couldn't be persuaded and neither could Wilma, and of course we all know why. To dutchman Mostert, Emily Hobhouse was a saint. Didn't she save his volk from being fed ground glass! Didn't she go round dishing out kindness to the Boerkie women and children starving to death in the concentration camps! Didn't she stand up in London to protest when the British burnt farmhouses and did that scorched-earth stuff!

And then I realized why he'd chosen Olive. It wasn't only the literature thing, it was because both Olive and Emily were pro-Boer. I ask you. With tears in my eyes, I ask you. Maybe he thought he was making some kind of reconciliation between Boer and Brit.

I've got nothing against Wilma, you understand. She does some strange things. But then look where she's coming from. Those are seriously strange people—and I'm not only talking about her parents. I'm talking about the dutchman in general. They've got enormous complexes about running around with bare feet and runny noses and being called bywoners. Okay, so they weren't all sharecroppers, but they've still got that mentality.

On the whole, though, Wilma was—sorry is—all right. She was a good wife to Christo, and that's not just being patronizing. I mean it, she was his friend. Maybe he kept some secrets from her, but then he built his life on those, always locking things away in drawers; so I'm sure there were some things he never told her. But I don't think he ever would've done anything to hurt her. He wasn't what you'd call besotted—who is after a few years of marriage? Yet I've no doubt he truly cared for her, no matter if things got a bit rocky sometimes.

I know she didn't like all his travelling and was probably concerned for his safety, and that must've led to some rows. Still, the marriage wasn't under any kind of threat, and so far as I can see was quite stable. Christo always said he wanted to make her life as easy for her as he could. Though he never thought that if he did something else, went back to law or something, he'd at least stay alive for her and the kids. He didn't think of that, the selfish bastard.

I'm sorry, Mr. Pole-ey, Mr. *Pooley*, I still get upset about what happened. Why would anyone want to do it to him! Christo was an honourable sort of guy. He didn't two-time people. If he made a deal he stuck by it. Oh Jesus. Oh Jesus, Jesus, Jesus. I'm sorry. I'm sorry. I didn't want to cry. I've been trying to psyche myself up not to, but I'm just a crybaby. I miss him dreadfully, you see. It's at moments like this I can understand why Wilma doesn't want to—won't—see you.

If the same thing happened to Ant [Anthony, her husband] I'd tell the press to go screw themselves. But it's not going to happen to Ant. He's just a stockbroker. Of course there's no saying they won't hijack him at a traffic light, but I've told him you just give them the keys and get out of the way pronto. For heaven's sake, they're armed with AKs these days. These blacks will shoot as soon as look at you. You know there're two or three hijackings a day in Jo'burg nowadays. It's frightening out there. It's a bloody war. Jesus, I tell you when Mandela goes I just don't know what's going to happen. It doesn't bear thinking about.

I'm sorry, what's that: Wilma? Oh yes, I was telling you about Wilma. In the beginning I think Ma and Dad were a bit offish towards her. Nothing rude, you understand, just sort of distant. And she was rather strange—awkward, you know, ill at ease. I don't think she liked coming over to visit us one little bit, but every Sunday Christo would bring her round for lunch. Ma used to do these roast numbers which weren't to be missed for the world, even though she overcooked the meat a tad.

Christo was living in Pretoria at the time, and probably not eating properly, knowing Christo. He hated cooking. You couldn't even get him to burn a sausage on the braai. Anyhow, there we'd all be and Wilma would be reticent—actually, not a goddamned peep out of her—and Ma and Dad would be offish and we'd eat in absolute silence. Can you believe it? We were all grown-up people—I must've been nineteen or twenty at least—and we couldn't think of a single word to say to one another. Sunday after Sunday we'd sit there sawing through the meat like Trappist monks. It's crazy the things we put ourselves through.

Anyhow, by the time they married things had thawed out a bit, and at least everyone was talking. But I still wouldn't say it was exactly happy families. Then again, I look at Ant's parents and there's no class thing dividing us, yet we're not entirely free of the occasional shouting match.

God alone knows how things would've progressed if Dad had lived. Probably he would've calmed down. All the same I had this scenario where he and the old dutchman would draw guns at one of those meet-the-in-laws lunches and start blasting away.

So that was—is—our Wilma. She and I didn't ever really hit it off, but it's not as if we had to live in one another's pockets. She just wasn't—isn't—my type. And I think, to be honest, she was a little jealous of my relationship with Christo. There were definitely things about him that I knew and she didn't.

Such as? Let me think. Such as Jorge Morate, for one. You won't know this, but Christo carried a crucifix wherever he went. He used to joke it was his good luck charm—so I guess its power suddenly ran out. Or maybe he wasn't carrying it up there. Anyhow, the point of the story is where he got it from, and that was Jorge Morate. Only Jorge Morate wasn't alive at the time; Christo'd just shot him dead.

This was in the bush war, you understand. He'd have shot Christo given half a chance, except at the time he wasn't carrying a gun. He'd just finished having a crap or something. Let me tell you, it got to Christo. He didn't stop playing war—I told you there was something perverse about him: it didn't stop him killing others—but he developed quite a thing about Jorge

Morate. He even talked about one day going over to Cuba to see where he'd lived. I personally didn't take that seriously. Christo had normally had four or five when that sort of stuff started coming out. And it only ever came out when we were alone. I never heard him talk about the bush war to anybody else. Probably not even he and Martin [Eloff] talked about it, and they were there in the same group or whatever you call it.

But just to get back to Jorge Morate for a moment. I think Christo told me about him when he got back from his first tour. He'd come home on a month's pass and didn't go out of the house once. He just stayed in his bedroom, most of the time in bed, and listened to Led Zeppelin and read these bloody Elizabethan plays. He was always reading. That's when it started his goddamned obsession with these damn plays. You'd think a person would get over that sort of thing at university. But not my Christo.

It drove Ma and Dad nuts. They wanted to scream and shout and tell him to stop acting like a child. I suppose they were worried. They knew something was wrong but didn't know what, and they certainly didn't know how to handle it. I managed to get them to lay off, tried to make them aware of what he'd been through, but they weren't convinced. If there was a bloody war up there, why wasn't anybody being told about it, my dad always argued. He could be so stupid sometimes. No political savvy at all. He just couldn't see that the last thing the government wanted was to tell everyone they were fighting a war, and Hey-ho, moms and dads, we want your sons.

So I'd spend time with Christo just sitting in his room listening to Led Zeppelin and not talking. He'd read; I'd do my studying. The records would go round and round. I watched the plays mount up. Marlowe, always Marlowe. A grimy copy of *Tamburlaine* was always lying next to his bed, and often with the crucifix on top of it.

Then one day he starts reading some of it into a tape recorder, so we stopped listening to Led Zeppelin and listened to his versions of Tamburlaine and Faustus and Edward the Second instead. He never stopped doing that, you know. He used to play his wretched recordings in his car. He was always quoting bits of the plays, and mostly people didn't know what on earth he was going on about. I used to wonder if he wasn't working towards being able to hold conversations made up of quotes from all those plays with not an original Christo Mercer sentence in them. He was completely cuckoo, and definitely needed therapy. But you can imagine what Christo thought of analysts. *Shrinks.* And nobody but madmen needed them, and he wasn't mad.

Except he *was* seriously disturbed. Jorge Morate had seriously disturbed him. And then Marlowe came along and seriously disturbed him some more. You know about Faustus, don't you? His contract with the devil and all that. Well, listen to this. Christo once advanced the theory that Jorge Morate was actually the devil, and that by killing him he'd contracted his soul to Lucifer. Jesus wept. Have you ever heard anything like it? And he thought he didn't need help. God alone. He had a serious problem and just refused to deal with it. And this was ten years later. In about 1985 or '86. I said to him, Christo, I've got the name of someone who can help you. And you know what he said to me? He said, Onions, Mary-lamb (that's what he called me, Mary-lamb), it's all onions.

It's a good question as to whether Christo ever had a twinge of conscience over what he did. For the most part I don't think so, certainly not in the early days. But after the elections, when the pressure really started and the Truth Commission was first suggested. . . . Well, I'm not so sure now that you mention it that it wasn't something like regret. Not that he ever said anything, so maybe it's just what I choose to believe. Maybe I want to think he had second thoughts because somewhere inside there was still something pricking at his conscience.

I don't know. I just don't know. Maybe it was why he got killed. Oh, shit. I'm getting into deep water here. . . . You're really making me stick my neck out.

[Long silence.]

Look, Mr. Poley, I'll tell you what I think. You can laugh at me if you want to, but this is my theory and I've got reasons for it. If you don't want to put it into your book that's your business. But if I don't say these things, who else is going to? And maybe in your investigations you may find something to back them up. But I'm warning you I've got no hard facts, just speculation.

Then again, Ant and I have talked it over so many nights that maybe we've now convinced ourselves it's the truth. I'll tell you one thing, though, I wasn't going to mention it because it makes us out to be conspiracy freaks. So first I want to assure you neither of us go around thinking the world's run by a Jewish cabal or the Knights Templar or the Rosicrucians or the Free Masons or anything like that, but you know how it is, sometimes there's just no other way to explain things.

[Pause.]

Okay, here goes. I—we, Ant and I—think Christo was killed by one of these "dirty tricks" guys. You know, the third force. Maybe he knew things about those high up, and what with the Truth Commission and the judicial inquiry into arms trading plenty of people were getting worried. Who knows what goes on in such circles. Maybe Christo was going to do a "Paul Erasmus," although I doubt it. But it would fit in with your theory that he was showing signs of remorse. I'd truly like to believe that, but in my heart of hearts I'm not sure I can. Christo could be a pretty hard bastard when he wanted to. By which I mean he's not the sort to have any hallelujah recantations. But that's it, I've said enough now. More than enough.

(Personal interview: Johannesburg; Tuesday, 3 October 1995)

Note 1: During my few days at the White Horse Inn on the outskirts of Johannesburg, I reread Louis Cohen's enthusiastic early-1890s *Reminiscences of Johannesburg and London* (Johannesburg: Africana Book Society, 1976), which always reinforces my prejudices about that wretched mining camp. "I do not think any town ever expanded more rapidly than did the Rand—it appeared to grow almost hourly, and newcomers of different nationalities came swarming into the place from all quarters. But apart from that, Johannesburg, although situated six thousand feet above the sea, was not in those early days a nice town to live in; it smelt like a farm of rotten eggs and was filthily dirty. When it rained—and didn't it!—the blessed village was submerged by fearful floods, and when dry it was hidden by the most terrible red, brown and yellow dust storms, born in the sanitary settlements, that were ever invoked by the devil. It is not to be wondered at that this foul dust caused much illness and many deaths. Although at times there was enough water in the town to float a ship, at other periods there was not sufficient to drown a flea—except at prohibitive prices—and a good, wholesome, liberal bath was generally out of the question. Some of the Anglo-Saxony tribe missed nothing they hadn't been used to."

Note 2: Khaki: "Boer name for a British soldier during the second Anglo-Boer War on account of the khaki-coloured uniform." Also "prefixed to several usually alien plant names, mostly noxious weeds: khakibos . . . said to have been introduced from elsewhere in forage or equipment for British troops" (*A Dictionary of South African English*).

Note 3: Mary Fitzgerald's reference to Christo Mercer's contact with the KwaZulu police force probably has to do with the training and arming of what have become known as SPUs (self-protection units). This led to an undeclared civil war between the Inkatha Freedom Party and the African National Congress. Death tolls of more than one hundred victims a week were not uncommon during late 1994 and throughout 1995.

The following extracts from a report in the *Mail & Guardian* of 22 September 1995 may well refer to the activities of International Ventures:

> Game reserves in remote areas under the control of the KwaZulu Department of Nature Conservation (KDNC) are being used to train members of the Inkatha Freedom Party's self-protection units, according to a report by the Network of Independent Monitors. KDNC executive director Nick Steele admitted that his department had been forced to hand over the Mlaba camp in 1994 so that it could be used for housing SPUs, but insisted that paramilitary activity was no longer taking place there.

Note 4: For those fastidious readers who are amenable to being sidetracked into the shadowy world of secret societies (so beloved by Enid Blyton), where men draped in sheets with holes cut out for their eyes gather in far-flung farmhouses to manipulate the fate of a nation, a useful book on the Broederbond is *The Superafrikaners* (Johannesburg: Jonathan Ball, 1978) by Ivor Wilkins and Hans Strydom.

Note 5: P. J. P. Mostert's friend Magnus Malan was appointed Chief of the Army in 1973 and Chief of the Defence Force in 1976.

As Chief of the Defence Force, Malan came into close

contact with P. W. Botha, who was Minister of Defence and later Prime Minister and later still President and then State President. Their views on politics and strategy coincided, and Malan states that Botha had a great influence on him. Malan's public statements as Chief of the Defence Force dealt mainly with the total onslaught against South Africa and the need to develop a total national strategy to counteract it at all levels, including military, political, diplomatic, economic, religious, cultural, sporting, and propaganda.

During this period the Armament Supply Organization (Armscor) became increasingly involved in the joint defence effort.

On 7 October 1980, Malan was appointed to the cabinet as Minister of Defence. He accepted the cabinet post feeling that he had fulfilled his aspirations in the Defence Force and that by playing a political role he could ensure continuity in the administration and future role of the military.

During his military career, Malan was awarded the following decorations: Star of South Africa, 1975; Southern Cross Decoration, 1977; Pro Patria Medal with Cunene Clasp, 1977 (extracted from Shelagh Gastrow's *Who's Who in South African Politics*, Johannesburg: Ravan Press, 1987).

A photograph taken by Paul Weinberg at a military parade in the mid-eighties shows Malan standing stiffly at attention, his hands gripped into fists. On his left is his admired leader, P. W. Botha. From the tiers of seats behind the podium a mass of dignitaries watch South Africa's might thundering past. Large and ominous in the foreground and cutting almost across the width of the picture is the barrel of a G6—Armscor's world-famous and much-purchased cannon. It rides just above the heads of Botha and Malan. Botha is taking the salute and his little porkpie hat is over his heart. Malan's porkpie is on his head; his face is cast in shadow. But the large prominent ears are clearly visible. He is not wearing glasses: his eyes are keen and unwavering. His mouth is a dark slit. Glanced at quickly, it could be a death's head beneath the hat brim.

On 2 November 1995, Malan and various generals were arrested and charged with orchestrating hit-squad activities which led to thirteen women and children being gunned down at KwaMakhutha in the early hours of Wednesday, 21 January 1987.

Not for nothing does Magnus Malan's name form the acronym Mal SA Gunman—which, I regret, is not an original but comes from the December 1995 issue of *Style* magazine, which I found lying in the reception room of my lawyers, Anziska, Friedman, Shapiro and Partners.

Note 6: On 24 October 1969, a French-built submarine sailed to South Africa. At the time the arms boycott had been in place for six years. The submarine would be called the *Emily Hobhouse* and was commissioned on 26 February 1971. It is still in operation. I think it's a perverse way of honouring a woman of peace, but so be it.

Note 7: Glass, death by eating thereof. This is a theme carried like a rumbling appendix in the bowels of some such as P. J. P. Mostert (and maybe this is where Christo Mercer got the idea for Sarra's death). It has its origins in a myth that those in the British Boer War concentration camps had their food "doctored" with glass on the express orders of their Herr Lager Kommandants. As thousands of the inmates succumbed to the dysentery shits, the story isn't inconceivable. It was supported by the prescription of epsom salts by camp medics, a laxative which probably only served to exacerbate the condition. Today the mythic remnants of this horror can be found on supermarket shelves, where epsom salts—its crystals resembling ground glass—is still labelled Engelse Sout.

Note 8: In his book *South Africa's Border War 1966–1989* (Gibraltar: Ashanti Publishing, 1989), Willem Steenkamp, who is notorious for his pro-SADF views but is currently the only published source, writes: "On November 20 [1975] an army patrol wiped out a 10-man insurgent gang after a mortar attack in which one soldier had been fatally wounded, and on November 26, four South African soldiers—two members of the permanent force and two national servicemen—were killed in a hot-pursuit operation, bringing the year's total of SADF operational deaths to 11." It is highly likely that Jorge Morate was a member of that "10-man insurgent gang." Estimates put the number of Cubans in Angola at about four thousand by November, and Steenkamp cites a figure of twelve thousand a month later.

Note 9: Paul Erasmus was a hit-squad operative active in the late eighties as part of the state's "dirty tricks" endeavours against dissidents. In the July and August 1995 issues of the *Mail & Guardian* he "came clean," as they say, although, like Lady Macbeth's damned spot, I doubt he will ever be able to wash this one away.

One of his revelations was that he suggested cleric Frank Chikane be put on the list for "permanent removal." Shortly afterwards Chikane's clothes were dusted with an organophosphate poison and the priest came close to dying.

A typical quote from Paul Erasmus' confession: "Not long after I joined the security police (in January 1977) I was told by my colleagues and superiors, including section head Major J. H. L. Jordaan and lieutenants At Kellerman (who later became President P. W. Botha's bodyguard) and Neville Els (who later became businessman and rugby lord Louis Luyt's bodyguard), that the monitoring of suspects included putting pressure on them, often in unlawful ways. This included acts like ordering unwanted supplies for suspects, killing their pets, throwing bricks through windows, and damaging vehicles." Sometimes, of course, it also included murdering them.

Note 10: The idea of a truth commission was first broached by the Minister of Justice, Dullah Omar, in May 1994 shortly after the first democratic elections had put a government of national unity into power. The concept caused a great deal of debate and only on 26 July 1995 was it signed into law as Act No. 34, the Truth and Reconciliation Act. In December 1995 the names of the Truth Commissioners were announced. Four months later the hearings began: so 1996 forever will be known as our year of truth.

23

This is a true story: I have no other way of presenting the facts.

When Christo Mercer checked into his London hotel—the Babington Court—on the afternoon of Saturday, 2 February 1991, there were four messages waiting for him. One was from his wife, Wilma, two were from his partner, Philip Kleinsmidt, and the fourth was from a Nicholas Skeres, who gave a London number. Christo Mercer slid this last back across the desk towards the receptionist.

"Are you sure this is for me?" he asked.

"Oh yes, Mr. Mercer," she replied. "That man called just two minutes ago."

Christo Mercer looked gloomily at the name: perhaps he'd been traced through Kleinsmidt, although he had expressly told him he was not going to England on business.

"For a break, Philip," he'd said. "For a three-day break."

"But we need you back here."

"Three days isn't going to make any difference."

"Wragtig, Christo! You and your bloody England."

Upstairs—in the room he'd so often used during the Precision Engineering days, with its reproduction nineteenth-century map of darkest Africa above the writing desk—Christo Mercer sat on the edge of the bed, covered his face with his hands, and dragged them down his long cheeks, stopping only when they shielded his mouth. He was heavy with fatigue. He didn't feel like speaking to anyone. He stared at the map, distracted, empty, his mind dulled. Gradually he realized the room was stale with the smell of cigarette smoke. Then he noticed, crushed in the ashtray beside the easy chair, the remains of a cigarette.

His first thought was to call reception, but the tiredness in him made it seem too much trouble; instead, wearily, he flushed the butt down the toilet and rinsed the ashtray in the basin.

In the last five days Christo Mercer had flown from Malitia to Khartoum, from Khartoum to Nairobi, from Nairobi to Tel Aviv (where he'd been shaken by Iraqi Scud attacks), and been taken by an agitated, angry captain Uri Izhar to see the devastation. They walked among the rubble: people stood in groups mesmerized by the rescue teams, the ambulances. He watched a soldier dig a dog out of a pile of bricks. The dog's back had been crushed, and it licked the man's hands, whimpering. For long moments the soldier stroked its muzzle, then he shot and the dog jerked twice and lay still. Christo Mercer turned away.

"One more of these," said Uri Izhar, "and we're going across there to take that mother out and to hell with Bush."

The next morning Christo Mercer flew from Tel Aviv on an empty El Al flight to London. He was relieved he didn't have to spend another day waiting for the missiles. He didn't want to hear—yet again—Uri Izhar's mad plans for retaliation. He wanted some peace in which to indulge his Elizabethan dreams.

London was grey and cold and damp and exactly the way he expected it. In the taxi from Heathrow, Christo Mercer looked out at Elizabeth's England—its traffic, its bustle, its houses and shops leaning over their narrow streets. The thoroughfares teemed with merchants, magicians, and porters, with horses, pigs, chickens, and dogs, with carts, tumbrels, and coaches; and over everything drifted the smell of dung, of smoke, of mud, of Spanish perfume. All so vibrant, yet it was a plague city, too. The crowds pushed up against the taxi, leering at him, offering for sale fish or eels or livers or Nashe's pamphlets or Dr. Dee's potions. Children among them held out live rabbits. Then he saw Christopher Marlowe and Thomas Kyd (the latter limping badly) cross the road before him, heading towards the Castle Inn, and he was still straining to peer out the rear window after them when the taxi pulled up at the hotel.

The fatigue of the real seeped back into him. Helpless against it, he paid the fare and carried his bag into the dim foyer.

Fifteen minutes later Christo Mercer spread the telephone messages on the bed and first called his wife, who was frantic with worry.

"I'm all right," he said. "Just tired."

"It's going to be another war, Christo," she said. "It's going to be another war."

"It's a long way away," he said. "Don't worry about it."

"Those Muslims are terrorists, Christo. They're going to put bombs on the Underground."

"Them and the IRA."

"Moenie grap maak nie. Allewêreld, Christo, it's not funny."

He spoke next to Philip Kleinsmidt, who told him the Jews had signed, that Uri Izhar was martial with outrage and armed beyond sanity. "So's everybody," said Christo Mercer. "See you Tuesday."

"Take the Sunday flight," urged Kleinsmidt.

"No," he replied. "Monday's soon enough."

Kleinsmidt didn't respond.

"And who's this Nicholas Skeres? What's he want?"

"How should I know!" said Kleinsmidt.

"You didn't tell him I'd be here?"

"No," said Kleinsmidt. "I've never heard of him."

When Christo Mercer phoned the number on the slip, the man who answered said he indeed was Nicholas Skeres but no there must've been some mistake as he'd never called the Babington. "How strange," Christo Mercer said.

"Isn't it," the man agreed. "I'm not sure whether someone's pulling your leg or mine."

Christo Mercer hung up, and shook his head as if to clear this strangeness away: though the name was familiar, he couldn't place it. Then he showered and changed and went out into the sunless afternoon. He was free in his London and for the next few hours nobody would know where to find him. He set off briskly to walk beside the Thames. He had an urgent need to see the river; he had to lean against the wall at the Embankment with the sun low in the clouds, diffuse and unreflected on the burnished water that inexorably slid, rippled, sibilant, hissing towards the Tower, where Kyd had once been tortured to denounce his friend Marlowe for heresy. The Thames was Christo Mercer's simplest link with Marlowe's world, for Marlowe, too, must have paused to stare at his thoughts swirling past with the driftwood and the weed and the discard of unknown lives.

Would it have been better to have lived then? Christo Mercer certainly thought so. Perhaps it was an age of violence and feud and capricious royal favour, but replace royal favour with presidential fancy and the description was as apt now as then. Royal agent. Government agent. Marlowe trading in software; he trading in hardware. There was common ground, similar experiences. Perhaps they could have been friends. Perhaps he could've been at Deptford with Marlowe and stopped Ingram Frizer's expert lunge with the dagger. Christo Mercer sighed:

elsewhere and other ages were always better. Which was why he never felt more at home than in London, and why he'd long suspected he'd been born out of his time.

As he moved away from the wall Christo Mercer bumped into a man whose stare was as fixed on the river as his had been. The man was standing very close yet he hadn't heard him approach. In the greying light they were the only people in sight engrossed by the Thames. Glimpsed from a passing taxi they might have been taken for friends, acquaintances, colleagues, conspirators, dealers.

"Excuse me," Christo Mercer mumbled as he brushed past, but the man neither spoke nor turned to look at him. He smelt of damp clothes and smoke. Not of cigarettes, but of open fires. Christo Mercer had the impression of a young man, and afterwards thought it was something about his naked hands on the wall—their rigidity, as if they were gripping a ledge—that had been the clue. But it was also the sapphire stud in his right ear and his hair caught back in a ponytail.

"Excuse me," he muttered again, and hurried off, his gloved hands punched deep into the pockets of his coat. Uneasy, he strode up Northumberland Avenue towards Nelson's Column. The pull of the river had loosened an anchorage within him, and for some reason he kept repeating the name Nicholas Skeres, Nicholas Skeres, like a mantra.

"Millions of souls sit on the banks of Styx," he said to himself. "Waiting the back return of Charon's boat."

He was exhausted, he counselled himself, simply overtired.

"Hell and Elysium swarm with ghosts of men," he recited, "That I have sent from sundry foughten fields."

He should take a taxi back to the hotel, where he could order room service and drug himself with television. Of course. As he crossed the Strand he glanced back, half expecting to see the young man following slowly behind, but among the tourists were no mysterious figures. Christo Mercer looked for a taxi in the heavy traffic.

"You're harbouring thoughts effeminate and faint," said the voice within. "How unseemly they are for our sex, our discipline of arms, the terror of our name."

When a taxi pulled up at the curb, Christo Mercer turned away and went on along St. Martin's Place. At Leicester Square the tiredness washed through him again. He stopped and stared at the blaze of neon and the glittering caverns booming with music: far from Elizabethan London, this was bright and mechanical and filled with inhuman noise.

He headed slowly towards Piccadilly. Among the crowds he glimpsed grand men in ruffs and cloaks, fine ladies, and scurrying fishwives, and he had to hold his nose at the stench of shit that came off the gutters. At a fast-food stand he bought a pizza wedge and stood away from the surge of pedestrians to eat it.

I hold the Fates bound fast in iron chains,
And with my hand turn Fortune's wheel about.

Outside a cinema he saw the young man again, and this time saw his face: the beard so sharply pointed at his chin, the thin moustache, the bulging steady eyes. The young man wore an army greatcoat and Doc Marten boots; he was looking away, but Christo Mercer knew that moments before those eyes had been watching him.

Nicholas Skeres, he thought. *You're* Nicholas Skeres. His smile made his lips turn down: he looked as sad as a tortoise.

Yet it was not until an hour later, when Christo Mercer stood gazing down at the contents of his briefcase spread so flagrantly over the bed in his hotel room that he called the young man sinister.

"So this is what your friends were doing while you followed me, my sinister Mr. Nicholas Skeres," he whispered. And then he stood for a long time wondering why this time, wondering who, wondering what he was being told, but no answers presented themselves.

Eventually he gathered and put back in the briefcase the papers, the pens, the calculator, his diary. He realized nothing was missing.

"You're just trying to scare me, aren't you, Nicholas Skeres?" he said out loud.

Although Christo Mercer didn't think his visitors would return, he couldn't bring himself to undress and go to bed. He poured a whisky from the minibar. He checked the locks on the door, then jammed a chair beneath the handle. This was ridiculous, of course, but precautions always looked ridiculous. He drained his glass and poured another drink and went to sit in the easy chair, where earlier in the day someone had sat and smoked a cigarette. Musing on the intrusion and the events of the afternoon, he could see no causal link between them. Yet he was unsettled.

Partly reading . . .

You that have march'd with happy Tamburlaine
As far as from the frozen place of Heaven

. . . partly listening . . .

We mean to travel to th' antarctic pole,
Conquering the people underneath our feet . . .

. . . as the hotel sighed and whispered and went quiet about him . . .

*Enter the Governor of Damascus, with three or four Citizens,
and four Virgins with branches of laurel in their hands*

. . . Christo Mercer eventually fell asleep in the chair.

He dreamt he was walking down a brightly lit corridor towards a door. The walls and floor were tiled, the ceiling unpainted concrete. He was carrying soup bowls on a tray. He opened the door—it wasn't locked—and went inside, then placed the tray on the floor. The room seemed to be a cell, dim and chiselled from stone.

A young girl's voice said, "Thank you."

He glanced quickly at her and noticed three other girls lying on a bench, shivering beneath their blankets.

He was tense and alert, his lips dry and slightly parted. The point of his tongue flicking across them quickly as a lizard. He unclenched his hands and the joints clicked. He stared at the girls, unclasped his belt buckle, unzipped.

"Look!" he shouted, and spat on his hand. His movements contorted his body, bent it, seemed to pull it inward until he reared grotesquely. His skin had gone metallic with sheen; his face was reptilian, his eyelids hooding and unhooding.

Christo Mercer woke with a start and rushed to the bathroom. He knelt at the toilet bowl and tried to retch, but the need was in his head, not his stomach. All he could do was spit into the water. He watched the bubbles slide across the surface and adhere to the porcelain, then flushed.

"Jesus, Christo," he whispered. "The torments and the hell."

He got up from the floor and stared at his waxy, porous face in the mirror. His eyelids drooped. His cheeks were bloated, and he needed a shave. The image of his shame couldn't be wiped from his mind. He was standing in the cell before those girls . . . it was disgusting. Revolting. Disturbing. And even worse, he wanted to carry on. And steadily he did.

At the end his stomach heaved, but again he wasn't sick. "Agge-nee!" he moaned, and stumbled back to the bedroom, dragging his jeans. He collapsed on the bed and crawled between the sheets. He still could see the girls cringing away from him.

And then he slept without dreaming for more than eight hours.

It was gone nine when Christo Mercer woke. Though the dream had faded, the residue of unease remained. As he lay rigid, staring at the map of Africa, he decided to change his flight. Once he'd made his usual pilgrimage to Marlowe's grave, there was nothing else to hold him in London. You can leave tonight, he told himself, and forget this nonsense. Get home to some sanity. He felt better then: the day had a plan, his actions a purpose. Confess, he continued, that this Nicholas Skeres scares you. His lips twitched downwards in their unhappy grin. He shook his head.

Later he made the necessary arrangements and phoned Wilma.

"Dis beter, Christo," she said. "The girls are missing you. I love you, skatlam."

When Christo Mercer entered the graveyard it was drizzling and as always the closing of the gate shut out the city's noise. He picked his way among the headstones to the near wall of the church, where the poet's name could be faintly seen among the lichen and the moss. The stone was so weathered the inscription grooves were almost indiscernible, but he believed he could make out some of the letters and, despite the cold, traced them with a bare finger.

Dead before thirty.

No one can make a truce with all the world, Christo Mercer said to the skeleton beneath the earth. After thirty it gets more complicated, Mr. Marlowe. No still points remain. No facts, no reality. Only a handful of illusions warring within our breasts for regiment. Perhaps it's better to be dead by thirty, when the world's still a solid place. I don't know, Mr. Marlowe. I fear we have lost the field.

Christo Mercer then walked away a few paces to search among the weeds for a small stone. He picked up a white pebble and set it on the slanting headstone. When it rolled off, he retrieved it and placed it more carefully on the rim. With the drizzle quickening, he went to stand in the lee of the church. Even though it was cold and wet, he wasn't ready to leave.

While he waited an old woman entered the churchyard and came arthritically towards Marlowe's grave, clutching against her chest what looked to be a small holly wreath. She was muttering as she approached, and her ceaseless commentary didn't stop while she circled the headstone. Christo Mercer watched her, could smell her scent of dried herbs and vinegar, could hear her thickened voice. With a brush of her hand she swept away his pebble of commemoration.

"Lord, Mr. Marley, there's no telling how these stones get up there and there's no use inquiring. Stranger things than that happen in this strange world of ours. But I'm not here to talk today. I'm not lingering in this drizzle so you'd best be grateful I'm here at all. Admit it, if it wasn't for Eleanor Bull there'd be no one to cheer up your spot in eternity. You'd long ago have been gone and forgotten and will be when they feed me to the worms. But until then, Mr. Marley, you're alive in the thoughts of Eleanor Bull. And grieved for. 'Tis such a waste what young men do. But they will argue and their daggers will come out quicker than their words. That's the way it is. Yet what it is makes poets keep bad company I'd never be able to say in a clutch of lifetimes. Lord rest you, Mr. Marley."

Earth, cast up fountains from thy entrails
And wet thy cheeks for their untimely deaths . . .

Note 1: In a true story accuracy is the first victim, which might sound like one of Professor Khafulo's aphorisms but in fact is mine. However, he did say: "The essence of truth lies not in facts, Robert, but in form. We're convinced not by what is said, but by how it's said. And sometimes, to arrive at a greater truth—something more truthful than what happened—our language forces us to, how shall I put it . . . invent? Yes. Invent: from the Latin, *invenire*, to come upon. In other words, narrative is a process of discovery. What we're talking about are the steps taken towards a truth. So these inventions aren't lies so much as explications" (21 October 1995).

Which is one way of looking at it.

Though it's a flight of fancy—no matter how necessary for Khafulo's "beauty of the form"—that Kyd was tortured in the Tower. He actually was tortured in Bridewell prison. In this instance I'll admit that torturing is the essential truth and that the place is incidental (especially so, I imagine, to Kyd), but I prefer to keep the record straight.

Quite what torments were done to him is not recorded, except that we know Her Majesty's Privy Council issued a quaintly worded general instruction to put those apprehended "to the torture in Bridewell, and by the extremity thereof draw them to discover their knowledge." In that process of drawing out knowledge he didn't know he had, Kyd suffered "pains and undeserved tortures"—to use his own words. Although he wasn't detained long, he died little more than a year later. Literary historians suspect he never recovered from the ordeal.

"Such, Robert, are the horrors of torture. And how often hasn't that story been repeated here! Biko *et al.*, RIP," as Professor Richard Khafulo commented (21 October 1995).

According to Kyd's interrogators: "Vile heretical conceipts denyinge the deity of Jhesus Christ our Savior, [were] founde amongest the papers of Thos Kydd, prisoner, wch he affirmeth that he had ffrom Marlowe." No doubt this betrayal of his friend came after he'd been hung from the manacles, had his nails torn out, his toes broken, or whatever.

Note 2: As a matter of interest, on the evening Christopher Marlowe was killed by Ingram Frizer, one of the three other men present was a shady youth with contacts in the underworld and in espionage. His name? Nicholas Skeres, of course. As always, I'm indebted to the Professor for this bit of information. "What else can I tell you, my dear Robert Poley?" Then in a broad smile which reveals an incisor missing from his right upper jaw: "You *will* acknowledge my input, won't you?"

Note 3: Graveyards just aren't my scene. Unlike another I could name (see chapter 37), I'm not in the habit of allowing goose-flesh to thrill up and down my arms while I stand at the last resting places of those tragically/brutally/unnecessarily slaughtered. Especially I see no sense in paying homage at Marlowe's grave. Marlowe means nothing to me and never has. But my journalistic instincts again insist that I highlight some inaccuracies that occurred in what Professor Khafulo calls "the text's elucidation of truer truths." Be that as it may.

Marlowe in fact was buried in an unmarked grave in the church of St. Nicholas, on the edge of Deptford Green, on 1 June 1593. This occurred immediately after the sixteen inquest jurors found Frizer had killed Marlowe "in the defence and saving of his own life." All that remains of this church from Elizabethan times is the north tower, and it is thought that the poet lies somewhere near it.

In the pursuit of these facts I asked Julia Clark, a friend of mine who was taking in the sights of London during December 1995, to visit the graveyard. She found the following on a plaque in the church wall: "Near this spot lie the mortal remains of

Christopher Marlowe who met his untimely death in Deptford on May 30, 1593." Beneath it is a quote from *Doctor Faustus*: "Cut is the branch that might have grown full straight."

The graveyard wall—one of those red-brick jobs covered in soot and moss—was probably built some one hundred fifty years ago. Mounted on each gatepost, an ominous skull and crossbones is a most grim message to us sightseeing mortals.

Of her excursion Julia writes: "Deptford is very Afro-Anglo (great shop on the High Street selling dried fish of all sorts + yams along with tacky African soap opera videos). The church itself is surrounded by tenement flats and semi-industrial buildings, but there are lots of beech trees in the churchyard and the bright green grass was sprinkled with their leaves. The gravestones are weathered and all the inscriptions have been worn away. The church was locked. There were planks in some of the windows + burglar bar meshes over all of them. Most of the gravestones were so white that they glared against the grass in the cloud-filtered light."

(Personal letter; 15 December 1995)

Note 4: There is no factual evidence or folkloric tradition that Eleanor Bull—or her bloody ghost—ever tended Marlowe's grave. Why should she? Even if he'd been killed at her establishment, it could just as easily have happened somewhere else, and it is only the fact of his death that links their names. So this is yet another example of *invenire*.

Note 5: "You will admit, Robert, I've been most discreet and haven't asked why you want all this information. But curiosity will out. Who *was* this Christo Mercer you keep mentioning?"

"You could call him a gunrunner, a death merchant."

"Ah! The ultimate cynic. A man with the courage of his convictions. I know you're not an art man, Robert, but have you never come across the work of a painter called Bacon? No! Such a pity. One of his pictures is of a howling pope, gripping his gold throne, his white robes flecked with blood, his mouth open in a scream of terror that I consider one of the central images of this century. It is truly exquisite, and speaks of everything we most fear. When you're next in New York promoting one of those"—he stirs his hands before him as if to cleanse a sullied word—"books of yours, you should try and see it." A sudden beam. "But now that's sidetracked me. . . . What were we talking about?"

"Selling guns."

"Oh yes, Francis Bacon. What I meant to tell you, Robert, was that somewhere Bacon said we—humankind, you understand—have finally realized we're an accident, that in other words, we're completely futile beings, with nothing left to us but to play out this senseless game of life—or words to that effect. Which I'll admit is a hard thought. But then it's not thought by too many of us, so the wheels of industry—or fortune—keep turning. But I wonder if it wasn't perhaps thought by your Christo Mercer! What do you think? You see, let me expand a moment. I think Marlowe's Tamburlaine knew this truth. So he might've called himself the scourge of God, but he wasn't out on any proselytizing mission. He's not God's avenging angel. He's out there slaughtering and conquering and subjugating—or so, at least, it seems to me. And as none of these activities are what you'd call nurturing affirmations of the essential goodness of the universe, one must assume that he had a pretty low opinion of human life. In short, Robert, he's a nihilist. That's why he kills virgins" (21 October 1995).

Note 6: Of England, Professor Richard Khafulo comments on this, his first land of exile:

"I must admit, Robert, that I have a lot of sympathy for your Christo Mercer's feeling for England. It rings true. I understand it. I understand it perfectly. London, you see, frozen, bright, clear-skied London was the first place I touched ground after I left South Africa. Certainly the plane stopped to refuel at Kinshasa, but they wouldn't let us out and so London was my first experience of the new world—at least my new world. It's a strange feeling, Robert, to go for the first time from the heat to the cold, from one end of the world to the other, in the space of twenty-four hours. It comes as a surprise to find you are able to breathe the air; that you can walk on the ground, maybe even can recognize buildings from photographs. A few things seem familiar, yet in all it's totally different. It might as well be another planet.

"You might want to know why I left the country, Robert, so let me tell you. In 1963, I was awarded a Rhodes scholarship to Oxford. Simply put, it was the greatest moment of my life. My mother and father couldn't believe it. They couldn't read what was written in the letter of acceptance, so I had to read it to them again and again. They cried with joy, were stunned with happiness. I shall carry the memory of their crying, smiling faces shining up at me to my death.

"It's just such a pity . . . no, never mind.

"Of course the next thing was I needed a passport. I went to town, got an application form. I filled it in, sent it to Pretoria, and then didn't think twice about it. But a month later I hadn't had even an acknowledgment. Two months later, still nothing. Now I was starting to worry. I went to ask at the Johannesburg office what was causing the delay, and they told me to be patient. I waited and waited. My parents became despondent. My father said the Boers would never give it to me. My mother said we must pray and that everything comes to those who wait.

Eventually, months later, when it was almost too late, the Department of Internal Affairs—or whatever it was called then—wrote and said my application had been rejected. They gave no reasons, and never did. But, ever so graciously, they informed me that on presentation of their letter I would be given an exit permit: a one-way ticket. Imagine this, Robert. I could go but they wouldn't let me return. I read the letter to my parents. Without hesitation my mother said, Go. Go, my father said. And so, like many others, I took the exit permit. When I was finally able to come back, my parents had been dead for ten years. I wasn't even allowed to bury them."

24

From my bedroom in the White Horse Inn, looking through a bright bougainvillaea onto the terraces where other guests were drinking chardonnay, I made a few phone calls. Some things are best handled by telephone. And this was how I chose to set up an appointment to see A. Kirkland, retired general and former director of Precision Engineering. After listening silently to my opening remarks, he said, "Jy's wat?"

I explained again that I was a writer.

"Vok off," he said. (And I might add that "fuck off" hardly captures the essence of the Afrikaans.)

With Philip Kleinsmidt, the remaining director of International Ventures, the telephone conversation was less cryptic but every bit as unhelpful.

"Mr. Poley, there is no point in you coming to see me because I have nothing to discuss with you. No, I'm not trying to hide anything. We're a private company. Our books are audited. We pay our taxes. More than that is none of your business. Yes, we have been implicated in the judicial inquiry into

Armscor, but then so have many other companies. The death of Mr. Mercer is deeply to be regretted. As you know he was the victim of a vicious mugging. These random events are always tragic. That's all I have to say. Goodbye. No. We no longer have any contact with John Campbell. Goodbye. What's that? Who's Nicholas Skeres? I've never heard of him before! Goodbye."

That same afternoon (Wednesday, 4 October 1995) I went to visit John Campbell, who lies dying of throat cancer in St. John's Hospice in the Johannesburg suburb of Orchards. He would not see me. A nurse told me he has a voice box but finds speaking very difficult. She described his condition with a flutter of her right hand which I interpreted as marginal, soon to be terminal.

25

Martin Eloff, Christo Mercer's long-standing friend, agreed to be interviewed on the condition that he could review the transcript and make any changes he deemed necessary. Although unhappy with this stipulation, I agreed on grounds that his contribution seemed vital. And in the end he made no significant alterations.

Eloff shared a tent with Christo Mercer during their tour of duty on the border and confirmed his obsession with *Tamburlaine*. He also said that he was well aware of his friend's clandestine gunrunning in north Africa, and that although Christo Mercer had stressed the delicacy of whatever details he told him, he held Eloff in such trust that he had no compunction about confiding in him. At least on most matters. Eloff, for instance, knew about Ibn el-Tamaru, but not that Christo Mercer could be found in his office manager's bed when he was in Malitia.

As a further requirement to this interview he insisted I state that he'd agreed to talk with me in order to correct some mis-information about Christo Mercer that had appeared both in the *Sunday Times* (in greatly truncated form) and in a magazine profile. The magazine, *Snatch*, lasted only for one issue, despite the large soft-porn market; the unbylined profile accused Christo Mercer of shooting dogs for pleasure while on the border, and of cowardice under attack. Eloff read this response onto the tape:

I want to state unequivocally that Christo Mercer was not among those who volunteered to shoot the dogs that had been given to soldiers by people living in northern Namibia. It is true that these dogs were shot because they had become a nuisance in the camp, and it is also true that the shooting was not done cleanly but in the manner of a massacre. Likewise it is true that the carcasses were sprinkled with petrol and set alight. Some of the dogs were not yet dead when this was done. Christo Mercer vigorously opposed this action and complained in writing to the office commanding. His letter would be on file in the company archives.

No one who served with Christo Mercer could accuse him of cowardice. On the occasion in question our unit was trapped under heavy fire on an island of thick bush in a dry riverbed. Our radio was broken, and there was no way of escaping without being shot to pieces. We were worried that the SWAPO forces firing at us would soon be backed up by mortars, which would have meant the end of us. When night fell Christo Mercer was among three men who volunteered to try and get help. He certainly did not run away, as the unnamed writer states. If it hadn't been for these three men it's likely that all fifteen of us—myself included—would have been killed.

I think it is important, Mr. Poley, for you to know the sort of friendship I had with Christo. To start with, we both enjoyed reading, although I could never really understand his fixation with the Elizabethans. However, he obviously found them truly fascinating. And then we were both poets.

Writing poetry is not something that is looked on with approval in the army, but Christo wrote some very fine verse both on the border and afterwards. I've no idea what happened to these poems. If his sister, Mary, doesn't know, then I suppose they're lost. And while Wilma may have them, I'm certainly not about to ask her to look among his papers. So if I were you I'd just pretend that they've been thrown away. I can tell you those poems were written in the best tradition of thirties Auden: the "Yes, we are going to suffer, now; the sky / Throbs like a fever-ish forehead; pain is real" sort of thing. But more than that I can't remember.

Apart from our time during national service, when you get to know somebody very quickly, especially when you have to trust people with your life, I was the best man at his marriage to Wilma, and I am godfather to both Olive and Emily.

In the early days before Olive was born, I spent two Christmases with them at his father-in-law's beach house at the Wilderness. And for the past twelve years Christo and I have met for lunch at least every two weeks. In addition to the times I went to dinner at their home.

I get on very well with Wilma. I feel deeply for her over what has happened, and it hurts me to see how badly she continues to take it. Christo was an easy man to love, Mr. Poley, and he has left an enormous gap in our lives. More than that I don't think I can really say. Perhaps you should give Tom Butera a call. They used to play squash together.

Yes, I would say Christo was a sombre individual. Dour is probably taking it a bit far, but he was not a man who laughed easily. He had no time for jokes. He couldn't even bear listening to them. So I suppose you could say he didn't have a sense of humour. However, there was one occasion when I suspect he played a trick, but it wasn't so much for the laugh as to humiliate this particular person.

The incident occurred in the war. We'd been out on patrol all day and were making our way back to camp. It was January or February, I don't remember exactly, but I do recall it was hot.

We came to this cuco shop—a little tin shack that sold beer and cold drinks. There were hundreds of these cuco shops in the bush and they did good business, not only with us but probably with the SWAPOs infiltrating through as well. I think they got their name from a type of beer that used to be brought down from Angola, but of course with the war that came to an end.

So when we got to this particular shop, all you could buy was Fanta orange or that sickly green cream soda. But it was cold, and we were hot and very thirsty.

I can't remember how many we had, let's say it was three or four each. So there we were, standing under the mopane trees drinking Fantas. It wasn't a big patrol, probably six of us. But our sergeant was a bastard, if you'll excuse my language. He'd been in the Reccies [reconnaissance troops, who had a reputation for savagery], he'd been in 32-Battalion [where the reputation was much the same], and somehow he'd ended up with us. He was a killer. He had a hard thin face and eyes that never seemed to blink. Completely mad. He was only happy when there was shooting. He treated us like dirt, probably because he sensed we despised him.

When we'd finished our drinks he decided to have a wee. Right there in front of the woman who ran the shop, he unzipped and started spraying the dirt. The next thing Christo did the same. I was amazed because Christo was highly discreet, and never did things like that. But there they were, side by side, wetting the ground in front of them.

Then Christo looks up and points and shouts and throws

himself to the ground. Without a thought, because that's the way we'd been trained, we all do the same. We lie there waiting for the explosion, but when nothing happens we stand up. And then we all burst out laughing—even the cuco shop woman— because the sergeant had dived straight onto the wet ground and, worse than that, he hadn't been able to stop his water.

Somehow none of this had happened to Christo. Christo stuck to his story about what he'd thought he'd seen, and there was not a thing the sergeant could do, although he swore and cursed and threatened to make us stand extra guard duties.

It may well be that Christo caught a glimpse of a circling ibis—there were always ibis near those shops, waiting for whatever offal was thrown out—or maybe he just made it up. I did ask him about it once, but he didn't even smile at the memory.

I thought you'd ask me about his death. I know it's led to all sorts of speculation about hit squads and such like, and no doubt there'll be a lot more when the judicial inquiry starts releasing its findings. Or when the Truth Commission hearings start. Personally, I don't think it has anything to do with the hit squads. Why should it? What Christo was involved in had nothing to do with the political struggle in South Africa. He was making money for the government, and he continued doing so when it changed from being Nationalist to this current gemors. You understand Afrikaans, Mr. Poley? Good. Then you appreciate that it means so much more than "mess."

Let me tell you two things. Christo was under enormous pressure after the change in government. Pressure to stop trading in arms because the ANC sat up in the clouds on the moral high ground. But Christo also believed that what he was doing was allowing oppressed people to gain their freedom. He felt that after their years of struggle the ANC should've been sympathetic to the causes he was espousing. They weren't, of course. Well, not initially. But that soon changed when they needed the money for reconstruction and development. By then it was too late for Christo.

I believe that when he went to Malitia he was what we'd call "clinically depressed." He might even have been in a state of mild schizophrenia and occasionally unable to make rational decisions about reality. I saw him for lunch on the Saturday before he left. He talked at length about the Marlowe play, and especially about Zenocrate, the wife of Tamburlaine. Though it wasn't unusual for us to speak about literature, this was bizarre. He had this crazy idea that of the four virgins Tamburlaine put to death she'd found one alive. That, he argued, would've altered the whole outcome of the play. To be honest, I couldn't understand what he was talking about. It seemed completely senseless.

Therefore, given his mental state and his crazy fixation with the play, I believe he committed suicide. Oh, I know he was killed, but I believe he provoked the attack. This was just the sort of thing he'd do. I witnessed this sort of behaviour on two occasions, up on the border, where he deliberately put himself into, quote unquote, "life-threatening situations." Christo had a death wish, Mr. Poley. The attack in Malitia was its manifestation.

(Personal interview: Pretoria; Thursday, 5 October 1995)

Note 1: In the seventies and early eighties, Christo Mercer had a number of poems published in literary magazines. One poem was even republished in England, which must say something, though quite what I'm not sure. Professor Khafulo (21 October 1995) sees it as an "example of the inevitable tension between the metropole and the periphery for those born on what the West views as the 'margins.' You could see it, Robert, as a crisis of identity."

Mary Fitzgerald concurs with the Professor. She believes her brother wanted to see if he was good enough for publication in the "metropole." Perhaps given his love of Elizabethan and, by extension, English literature, there must be some truth in this. But we'll never know.

Fortunately, Mary kept copies of the journals where the work appeared and, as she is more or less his literary executor, gave me permission to reproduce them here. I also went to the trouble of scanning other contemporary "little magazines"—which the Professor assured me is what the aficionados called them. However, among a profuse outpouring of anguished verse—most of it appallingly bad, and I mean awful, even I could do better—the name of Christo Mercer is not again to be found.

This, of course, does not mean that he wasn't writing. In fact, the Professor informs me that, based on the superior level of technical skill shown in the crafting of Christo Mercer's last poem, "In a Rhodesian Garden," it can fairly reasonably be concluded that he must've kept at it throughout the seventies even if he chose not to publish. "'Rhodesian Garden' is actually rather good" were his exact words. Apparently he bases this opinion on word usage, imagery, metaphor, and rhythm, which he judges "succinct, accomplished." It's the only poem Christo Mercer published after his student years. In a world of significant details, this one might be especially so.

In further support of this speculation, Mary Fitzgerald says her brother told her he wrote a large number of poems on his return from the bush war. None of them was published, or at least not under his name. In my discussions with the Professor he told me it was not uncommon for writers to use a variety of pseudonyms during their careers: a variation on the Was-Shakespeare-really-Marlowe? theme. This in turn creates valuable areas of academic research for future PhD students.

However, I digress. Christo Mercer's first poem is a short piece written at university in response to, presumably, a mention in a lecture of Sylvia Plath's suicide. I'm also told that it shows the influence of her work. Despite its technical clumsiness—"the multi-syllabic inappropriateness of the word 'occasional,'" for example—the poem reveals a fascination with death and a rather romantic attitude towards what one might call the agony of the human heart. This, at least, is my interpretation. More importantly, the first line could have been an epitaph for Christo Mercer's life. There is ample evidence, for instance his obsessive late-night fascination with *Tamburlaine*, to suggest he was no stranger to what he calls here "the small and lonely hours." Once again, this is merely my exegesis.

The poem was published under the name Christo E. Mercer in *New Coin*, Vol. 8, nos. 3 & 4, November 1972. He later signed his work Christo Mercer. Christo, his sister reminds me, was a childhood nickname.

IN THE SMALL HOURS

> *In the small and lonely hours*
> *Visited only by occasional cars*
> *She wrote the long, thin cries.*
>
> *When husbands and wives*
> *Move restlessly between the sheets,*
> *A sour taste clutched her tongue;*
>
> *Her art ended. Into these hours,*
> *Perfect and sweet, her poisoned lungs*
> *Exhaled gas amongst the flowers.*

Between 1972 and 1974 a rash of poems appeared in the university literary journal *Critique*. Mostly these are suburban laments or what the Professor refers to as "Larkinesque depictions of life as ennui and malaise." This, it seems to me, is the stuff of standard student fare. On the whole they're ghastly.

However, one poem does bear mention. It's called "Fish Tank" and written in what I'm told is called the "confessional style of Robert Lowell." The opening couplet reads:

> *Still, in the blue of the fish tank light,*
> *I sit alone and pass the night.*

Yuk! "Fish Tank" is emphatically not a good poem, and here, I must say, I don't require Professor Khafulo's learned judgments. Even I can hear how brutally the rhymes jar. This does not, however, stop it from being significant in Christo Mercer's oeuvre, if that's not too grand a word. For these three reasons: it returns to the theme of late-night angst; it displays a profound disillusionment with society (a common topic in any student verse); and it goes one step further by suggesting, perhaps even advocating, war. This last intention, however poorly expressed, implies that society is in such an advanced state of moral degeneracy as to deserve obliteration. At least that's the only sense I (or the good Professor) can make of these ham-handed lines:

> *The people in the cinema queue*
> *Have all gone home. Too few*
>
> *Understood what it was they saw.*
> *Who am I to talk of war.*

"Really, this is just too awful," was Professor Khafulo's assessment of the poems' aesthetic merits.

But my question in turn was: what misunderstood movie is he referring to?

This gave him pause, but then he beamed. "Of course. Can't you see? It's so obvious."

My blank look persevered.

"Come now, Robert, you're a journalist. You should know how to put two and two together."

Ah, such a flattering opinion of journalists.

"It's *A Clockwork Orange*, of course."

"How in the world did you work that out?"

"Well, my dear Robert," he said, "there's a clue in the very next couplet."

> *The last bars of the Ninth Symphony*
> *Are still tapped out upon my knee.*

Apparently, in Anthony Burgess's "compelling" novel it was Beethoven's Ninth that switched on the young gangleader Alex. The music was also used in Stanley Kubrick's film, though at the time (1971) the film was banned in South Africa.

As I happened to know, and explained to my instructor. "So it couldn't have been that movie!" I triumphantly concluded.

"It's a case of literary licence," he retorted. "We're dealing with a poem, not a newspaper article. [Though I also happen to know that newspapers not infrequently employ considerable poetic licence.] So we must not dismiss the fact that your poet may well have read *A Clockwork Orange*, which still is a popular book with students, and is conceivably merely *alluding* to the film."

This is a tantalizing argument, especially as it describes the sort of war our narrator is thinking of: internecine, random urban conflict. And certainly the end of the sonnet could be taken as a measure of how deeply Christo Mercer identified with Alex.

In the tank the sunken wreck
Has snails crawling on its deck

And silent fish amongst the green
Who cannot know what I mean

By smashing in their world
Leaving them hard and curled.

I ask you: what sort of editor would publish this crap!

However, hear out Professor Khafulo: "This final sestet presents a world where ordinary creatures go about their ordinary business—a reference to the people in the cinema queue—and then, suddenly, it's destroyed. [Much as the warlords Christo Mercer supplied wrought destruction on the lives of ordinary people.] Violence is shown to be easy, and perhaps necessary, once society becomes stagnant. There is, I find, a disturbing satisfaction in the tone of the final line, which can only be explained as an endorsement of destruction. Nor would it be beyond the bounds of interpretation to say the narrator [or the poet!] took a sadistic pleasure in such apocalyptic images."

"Fish Tank" was published in a not-quite-liberal sociopolitical monthly called *New Nation* in August 1972. The editor was none other than Denis Worrall, who was, for much of the eighties, to be State President Botha's ambassador to the Court of St. James.

As I've noted, Christo Mercer's name wouldn't appear in print again until 1979. When it does, it is above a poem so completely different from his student verse as to pose a number of interesting political and biographical points.

The first is that the poem's subject is Rhodesia in the late seventies, when the war was at its most desperate, when to all but the singularly obtuse the end must've been evident. (Rhodesia became Zimbabwe in 1980.) As far as I can establish, Christo Mercer never visited Rhodesia, much less Salisbury or Meikles Hotel and its famous bar. Yet the narrator records a pop song—"Sweet Bananas," not an invention—being played over the bar radio for the troops. I recall its popularity there at that time because I was covering the pre-independence talks and spent many hours at the Meikles.

This leads to a second comment, this one based on the good Professor's literary explication: the poem smacks of personal experience. "The poem is constructed on a series of observations which carefully set about creating a sense of place. These are very specific, even down to the types of trees in the suburban gardens."

In other words, his details supply a sort of information that suggests at least some familiarity with Rhodesia. Moreover, the voice of the narrator, who takes the liberty of speaking for the white citizenry, has a ring of authenticity about it.

As far as I can see, none of these feelings would be above any writer who'd visited the country, but in a very real sense Christo Mercer was not a writer. He conceivably wrote many more than the clutch of poems we know of, but that, at the end of the day, makes up his entire imaginative output. (The dream fantasy and his monograph on Marlowe are of a different order.) So Christo Mercer either had a moment of inspirational serendipity in writing this piece or actually had visited this country.

If he had, this probably would've been in 1978. The poem appeared in the magazine *Staffrider* (Vol. 2, no. 3) in mid-1979; given that it would represent at the very least a few nights' work, and that it might have been accepted for publication a good six months before it appeared, then it most likely was written towards the end of 1978.

At the time Christo Mercer was working for his father-in-law's legal firm but was only a year away from his move to Precision Engineering. South Africa then was heavily committed to supplying Ian Smith's regime with arms and fuel in defiance of international sanctions against the Rhodesian government. The question begs: is this where Christo Mercer began the career that was to end his life? Both Mostert and his daughter could answer this question, but they won't.

A final (personal) observation about the poem: it probably echoes Christo Mercer's experience in Angola, given the constant references to the effects of war and, to quote my man in the Ivory Tower, "a very strong feeling that a way of life is coming to an end permeates every line."

The poem also captures a fear that was not uncommon in white South African households. In the late seventies, when political unrest was fomenting in the townships, many were wondering if they, too, would become "unpitied refugees."

I'm forced to ask: is there any irony at work in this piece? Does it express a warning? The answer to both questions, it seems to me, is Yes. Certainly the last line is loaded with irony. But if that's the case, these are strange opinions to be held by an arms dealer, a type not known for moral imperatives.

Three years after this poem was published in *Staffrider* it appeared in *London Magazine* (Vol. 21, no. 12, March 1982).

IN A RHODESIAN GARDEN

It is August and the months are closing.
War rattles in the provinces, bombs
Blow out in cities. There is talk
Of peace and more murders in the bush.
Some leave and do not return. Once
Were proud funerals and a sharp salute;
But now only the empty prayer,

The smiling photograph upon the dresser.
It is August and the days are numbered.

The garden is our latest retreat:
The blue gums along the fence,
The purple wisteria in bloom above the stoep.
Our happy days still haunt us.
This hour when light is mauve and warm,
The birds quiet and a drunken bat
Careens above the lawn, once held us
Perfectly. I can see it all: the house
Against a draining sky, a couple
In garden chairs upon the grass.
One room is lit: behind thick curtains
A houseboy sets the knives and forks.

That time is over. Now soldiers lurch
In Meikles' bar with tales of villages
They burnt to get the truth. We talk
Our cocktails dry of friends on farms:
The tobacco fields untended, the dog
Found dead outside the kitchen door.
All swings about these points: the war
Is closing, the roads dangerous . . . but hear,
They're playing "Sweet Bananas" for the troops.

It could have been paradise on earth.
Behind our eyes windows look down valley
From farmhouses where sunlight slides across
Abandoned afternoons. We will never live there again.
Here we play out the closing of a world
At tennis or bridge, sweating slightly
In the heavy air, always cordial,

Always beyond hope and despair:
Hearing of one northbound, while
Someone else is leaving for the south.

The times are against us. We are still
Strangers here, but nowhere else is home.
Can it be we were wrong about the country?
That it was ever just outside our reach:
Only a conjectured colony,
A coloured piece upon an office map
From which we'll run unpitied refugees.
No. It cannot be imagined without us.

Note 2: On my answering machine (Tuesday, 24 October 1995): "Hello, Robert, Richard speaking. Well, here's a truly extraordinary piece of good fortune. Certainly worth you standing me a drink, I'd say. That Auden 'pain is real' reference is not to be found among *The Collected Poems*, and in fact it seems Auden excised it from his China sonnets. Instead you'll find it on page 256 of *The English Auden* (London: Faber and Faber, 1977), specifically sonnet XIV of the 'In Time of War' sequence. How's that for detective work? Do call to congratulate me. Ciao for now."

Note 3: Lives of the Poets: Sylvia Plath gassed herself in 1963. Robert Lowell behaved outrageously with women. And Larkinesque is, of course, a reference to the eponymous Philip who wrote that sexual intercourse, beginning only in 1963, came too late for him. "Absolute nonsense," according to the Professor. "Larkin sometimes had two women on the go. He was also a purveyor of soft porn, so he was probably a frequent masturbator as well. As was Dylan Thomas, I'll have you know."

Fascinating stuff, this.

Note 4: Two items from far-flung correspondents. First Professor Khafulo (again): "You're an interesting man, Robert. And I'm deeply intrigued by this little project of yours. Why don't we get together for a drink sometime soon" (21 October 1995).

Second, Justine: "It's time you came out of the closet, Robert. Admit it, you're not interested in pussy anymore" (14 July 1995).

26

For no reason other than the hell of it I contacted the squash-playing Tom (Tommaso) Butera:

Look, I don't want to get mixed up in this. I played squash with him once a week. I didn't know what he did until I saw his name in the paper. I thought it was awful when he got killed, but these days you're not safe anywhere.

No, I'd never been to his house. I hadn't met his wife. I knew nothing about his business. Obviously I knew he travelled a lot, but so what? I mean, the planes are full of businessmen.

Sure, after we'd had a game we went to the McKintys down the road for a beer, but you can't make a conspiracy out of that. It was just two guys having a beer and talking about sport or something. That's all. I wasn't a friend of his. Just leave me out of this, okay?

And don't start that stuff about my name. I was born in this country. I'm a chartered accountant. Working for my uncle doesn't mean I have anything to do with the Italians. I've never even been to Sicily.

(Telephone interview; Friday, 6 October 1995)

Sometimes the leads go nowhere but it's always fascinating hearing what people have to say!

27

Florence Mercer is seventy-one years old and lives in an old-age home called Lentegeur, which translates as something like "the scent of autumn"; the only scent in Port Elizabeth, however, is that of Karoo bush on waste ground near the airport, and it's as pleasant and sharp as cat's piss. Port Elizabeth's a long way from Pretoria and Johannesburg, though to Florence Mercer perhaps the distance separating her from her family doesn't matter much. She is no longer strongly connected to reality—a fact drawn to my attention by Mary Fitzgerald. Nevertheless, I had to see the old lady.

Like so many elderly women in these places, Florence Mercer sat in a chair in her room and wore a light cardigan despite the heat of the day. The windows were closed. She certainly won't smell any scent whatsoever even when autumn comes. She was watching television. On her bedside table were photographs of Christo and Mary as young children. Hanging on the wall in a single frame were snapshots of her grandchildren and of her son and daughter and their spouses.

I was shown up to her room by the matron. I already had the tape recorder running, so this surreal conversation was duly recorded.

"Mrs. Mercer, someone to see you."

"Has he come to fix my television?"

"Your television's not broken, Mrs. Mercer. Look, it's working perfectly."

"Sister Morris said she'd get someone to fix it."

"Then I'm sure someone will come and fix it."

"Has this man come to fix it?"

"No, Mrs. Mercer, this is Mr. Poley from the newspapers. He's come to talk to you about your son."

"Ah, not exactly, matron. I'm a writer, but I don't work for a newspaper. I write books."

"It's not the same thing?"

"No. Not at all really."

"Oh, I always thought it was. But never mind. I'll come and see how you two are getting on in about twenty minutes."

"My television's not working properly."

"I'm afraid I don't know anything about television, Mrs. Mercer. I was wondering if you could tell me about Christo."

"I'm going to Christo for Christmas. I always go up to Christo for Christmas. It's nice to have the whole family together. Sometimes they've come down here, but usually it's too windy on the beach, at least in the afternoon. I spend a week with Christo and a week with Mary. I like to get away. It's very nice here Mr.—what did you say your name was?

"Poley."

"A man is coming to fix my television. But that's not you, is it?"

"No. I'm writing a book about your son."

"That's nice. I suppose the television man will be along shortly."

I cough. The remains of a spring cold have settled in my chest.

"Christo always uses onions for a cough. I don't know where he gets these ideas from sometimes. Perhaps it's all those books he's always reading. I used to give them Stern's Pine Tar and Honey when they had coughs and then one day Christo says no, I must start using onions. I've got to slice the onions and sprinkle them with brown sugar and leave them overnight. And the next morning he drinks the juice. He made his sister drink it too. She's always hated the taste of onions."

"Do you remember when Christo first started writing poems?"

"Christo never smoked. Jack smoked a pipe. I think the tobacco was called Seaman's Blend with rum extract. I always thought it gave the house a wonderful aroma. But Christo doesn't smoke. He's not like other boys his age. You see a lot of smoking on television. That's why there's so many young people who smoke. Thank you so much for fixing my television, Mr. Poley, I don't like missing 'Surgical Spirit.' It's my favourite programme."

(Personal interview: Port Elizabeth; Tuesday, 10 October 1995)

Jesus bloody Christ!

28

Back in Cape Town—showered with giggles and spit and happiness by Omar Sharif and Bette Davis (especially after I gave them money for booze), shouted at by Justine (who didn't want to hear me talk about khakibos), hounded by the Elizabethan expert, and avoided by Luke—I phoned Mary Fitzgerald to inquire about onions:

You know, it's strange you should ask because Christo had a big thing about onions. I can't remember exactly when it started, but I guess it must've been sometime during his national service. Maybe they served so much fried onion that he just got sick and tired of it. Although, as with so many things with Christo, when he got sick and tired of something he'd just go off it completely. Wilma never had an onion in the house. He could smell them a mile away. I'm exaggerating, of course, but you know what I mean. And all this from someone who loved onions as a child.

I remember he used to eat raw onions. As my kids would say, it was gross, man, gross. By God, his breath smelt. As a boy he had this gang, and you could join only if you ate a raw onion. I wanted so desperately to belong but I could never eat an onion and Christo wouldn't bend the rules for me.

Once, I don't know when it was, probably when he was at high school, he got this crazy idea about making cough mixture from raw onion juice and sugar. He must have read it in some magazine or something. And it sure worked for him. But when I got a cough he made me drink some and I puked it was so foul. So I was really amused when Christo went off onions, even cooked.

(Telephone interview; Thursday, 12 October 1995)

29

Ditto call to Martin Eloff:

I had no idea Christo didn't like onions, Mr. Poley. As far as I can remember he wasn't a fussy eater. Really, this is a very strange question. I can't see why it would possibly be of interest.

(Telephone interview; Thursday, 12 October 1995)

30

Some days later Mary Fitzgerald called me:

Hello, Mr. Poley, this is Mary Fitzgerald. Sorry not to catch you, but it's just a small thing I've remembered so there's no need to phone me back. Remember you asked me to phone you if I thought of anything relevant and, well, I've just thought of something that I don't know why I didn't think of before. It's so obvious, really. It's about that onion business. A bit gruesome, not at all the sort of thing one needs on one's answering machine, but here goes anyhow. This has to do with that guy

Jorge Morate, who Christo shot. I told you how Christo went back afterwards and took his crucifix and searched for his documents. Well, while Christo was going through his pockets, the corpse sighed—I don't know why, maybe the lungs collapsed or something—and this waft of onion breath blew out. It was enough to make Christo hurl. I can only think this is why Christo went off onions. Once again, my apologies for leaving such a macabre message.

That's it, really. Thank you. Cheers.

(Telephone message; Monday, 16 October 1995).

PART IV

Reconciliation

31

I am no traveller. I don't visit foreign places. I'd never go within a hundred miles of any war. Unlike Martha Gellhorn, I would have felt no compulsion to be in Prague in 1938 when the Gestapo net spread through the Sudetenland. Yet I decided to go to Malitia.

Partly I went because the journalist within me felt a need for some kind of truth, and partly to escape Justine's madness (her lover had moved in with her). Also I had to get away from our boys: Matthew and particularly Luke were tearing at my conscience. Luke's world had disintegrated further still and turned very weird. He was plugged into hate tapes by Nine Inch Nails and went around singing about rape and the joy of shooting holes in women's heads. He was probably smoked up most hours of any given day.

I was running away, yet who isn't? So I followed Christo Mercer to Nairobi, but couldn't get a flight to Mogadishu because no one would dream of flying there. Mogadishu was a war zone again. Instead I had to go to Khartoum and spend a long night at the Hotel Acropol, restless beneath the sheets. With no hope of sleep, I read in irritable James Wellard's *The Great Sahara* about the evils of humankind:

> In fact, what with the sufferings of the Africans driven north-wards to slavery, the horrible fate of the salt-miners, the tor-ments of thirst endured by the caravaners, the terror of the

dwellers in the oases subjected to continual raids by the desert bandits, not to mention the misery of the overladen and exhausted beasts of burden, the history of the Sahara trade is neither romantic nor pleasant. In a sense it is further debased by the ruthlessness and cruelty of the Arab bosses who controlled it from earliest times, since Islam always encouraged and gave religious sanction to slavery. About all that can be said in excuse, if an excuse it is, is that Christians exploited and profited from the same trade for 400 years during which the captive Africans were shipped out of the Slave Coast port by the tens of thousands.

The next morning I took what must have been the last Dakota left on the planet out over the endless desert, bound for Malitia. Not a restful flight, you might say. There were five of us paying to fly in that rattling relic and we all served up our breakfasts. I wondered what sort of stomach Christo Mercer had had for these damn contraptions.

For more hours than I care to remember I watched the unchanging brown below, on which nothing seemed to live. Scarred brown beds where rivers once had flowed, sometimes with a glint of blue metal but mostly just the brown. I leant my forehead on the cold window and cursed Christo Mercer for the remoteness of his death.

In my mind Justine said, "You're losing your grip, Robert. There's no such place as Malitia. Grow up. Accept your crappy fate."

Near Malitia, oil derricks burnt like metal candles. Slowly the plane came down. On the outskirts the tin shacks exuded constant smoke. Here people scraped at the gravel using blades of tin: the women with babies tied to their backs; the men in a frenzied hacking; young children carting rubble to the mounds. Later I was told that they were prospecting for gold, yet none of these would ever be rich. The money went to those who owned the concessions, so the poor would die in the pits and holes they dug or go back to their villages with their lungs in shreds. But do not pity them, I was told, because they have their dreams.

It was dreams this city of Malitia cherished, dreams of money. The beggar wanted not food but money. The rich demanded cash and would give no credit. Here, where everything had value, everything was for sale; every body, every thought, every emotion, every object had its price, even conversations. Words, particularly, were expensive, the whispered ones the most dear of all. This was a city of suspicion. Of threat. Of fear. This was the city where Christo Mercer sold his guns.

From the rickshaw taxi I watched the sun go down through the haze and knew the desolation of the traveller, a stranger in a foreign place at night. The driver cycled without pause into streets of scooters and wild noise and lights and screeching faces. A woman lay convulsed beside the road, jerking as a fit shot through her, foaming. We passed by. Others passed by. No one stopped.

We raced on through a labyrinth of these loud anonymous streets until, swinging out of the maelstrom, we lurched into a sudden quiet: a dim lane without traffic. Above an open door was the name Pigalle Hotel (kindly recommended by Deep Throat II). Inside, I was shown to a room: a bed, a table, a bare floor, an open window, from the ceiling a shaded bulb hanging on a long cord that swung in the breeze, throwing shadows over the walls and across the floor.

I sat down on the bed. These are the moments that most disturb me. The loneliness. The aloneness. It is at such moments your life rushes at you the way the horsemen charged the four virgins. Their lances went in; I bled.

It's like this, at least to me it seems like this: last July, Justine went out one morning (the fourteenth, I'll never forget that date) to her architectural practice as my loving wife and came back a gorgon. And truly I was turned to stone. She stood before me with serpents in her hair, her fingers trying to claw out my eyes, and I was turned to stone. I looked at her and didn't know who she was. Matthew and Luke ran up the volume of their frightening music to drown out their mother's frightening rant but I was transfixed, petrified.

All that we had lived for, all that we had built, was crashing down around us—literally, in some instances, as she smashed crockery, threw expensive sculptures through plate-glass windows, destroyed an entire heirloom of porcelain figurines her mother had left her (this last, I must confess, was something I'd long craved doing). In those moments our sons' well-being, our insurance installments, pension plans, almost paid-up mortgage, cars, Jersey Island bank account, and in fact our entire future were rendered unto dust. Or, rather, shards of porcelain and glass, bits of paper, even crumpled metal (after she stomped the amplifier and CD player).

"Get a life, Robert," she screamed. "We're too young to be dead."

At her forty-eight and my forty-three she had a point.

Then she drank three mouthfuls of whisky straight from the bottle and disappeared into the night.

Matthew and Luke had the good sense not to come out of their gangsta-rap heaven. Surely the sight of their father crying would've bewildered them no end.

And so to maudlin self-reproach.

I'll admit I'd sunk into some slovenly ways. Saturday afternoons watching sport on television. More beer than I should've consumed. Stomach beginning to bulge. But at least I'd quit smoking. Okay, we hadn't been on a decent holiday for two years, but that's partly the ever-so-hard-working Justine's fault. Yes, I spent hours writing my best-sellers and my off-time didn't always coincide with hers. So we didn't go out more than once in a blue moon. No, I can't remember when last we had a supper that wasn't take-away pizzas from Moma's at the shopping mall. Of course I'd rather watch videos than stand in line for a movie. Maybe I sometimes didn't change my underwear for two days running, though even this beats the British average. I don't always shave every morning, either. And if we hadn't made love for the better part of six months, it does take two to tango.

But are these compelling reasons to make a successful architect grow snakes in her hair? Compelling enough to make her run for solace into the arms of a dyke? God help us!

What *has* this woman got? I've seen her, and mostly she looks like David Bowie with short black hair. She can't be more than thirty. Plus she smokes, and Justine can't abide cigarettes; she bites her nails and Justine hates fidgeters; her wardrobe extends no further than T-shirts and jeans, and Justine wouldn't be caught dead in Levi's; she raves the night away, and until last August Justine couldn't have guessed what Ecstasy was. This woman, if that's what she is, this bitch—naming her would only make her real—has a professional middle-aged woman, the mother of two sons, crawling all over her body doing unspeakable things. The mind boggles. For Christ's sake, what has this Ziggy Stardust knock-off got to offer my fucking wife!

I have tried to put myself in Justine's shoes. But for the life of me I can't understand. As a respected architect she's in great demand—and boy, does she earn! She has a twenty-year marriage. Her husband never played the field! She has two teenage sons. We all appreciated her, and she didn't even have to clean our mess (Maria handles that). In our strange ways we love her. *I* love her, even now. I think. Or at least what I'd call love: caring, concern, interest. I thought we were happy. Up until the day she metamorphosed I'd thought we were happy. We had our differences, of course, as everybody does, but we could still laugh together. We hadn't argued in months. She had all the material goods she might desire. So why did she turn into a gorgon? What worm of despair found its way into her heart? I have no idea.

There's no point to this. After twenty-one years I still don't know her. I have to admit Justine is as much a stranger to me as the day we met. No, actually it's worse. I know things about her: that she never sleeps late even on holidays, that she fears spiders, that she suffers pollen allergies, that her menstrual pains double her up, that she'll go all night when she's in the party mood, that she can organize the impossible. I know what flowers she likes (arum lilies), what perfume (Miss Dior, Chanel No. 19), her favourite fruit (strawberries), her sort of books (biographies), her chocolate (Côte d'Or dark, Terry's Oranges plain), her weight (65 kg) and bra size (38B), what menstrual pads she buys (Always Ultra Plus), her thoughts on abortion (pro), her politics (Democratic Party). I know she's anti hanging, testing nuclear bombs, whaling, culling elephants, presidential pardons for rapists. I know what styles of architecture excite her (Pompidou centre, glass pyramid at the Louvre) and why she despises municipal officials. Sometimes I can even anticipate what she might say. I know all these things, after living through twenty years with her: an idea of Justine, reinforced, supported, collaborated by no less a person than Justine herself. And yet inside Justine was always the gorgon waiting for the empowering hormone imbalance. I can't call Justine a stranger; it's worse than that: she has become someone else.

There's also this: if I didn't know Justine, what don't I know about myself? Frightening. Maybe it was a lack of self-knowledge that scared Christo Mercer. It's not so much what seem to be sudden changes that alarm us but the realization that nothing's really changed, that we've just been given new information. That the earth's not the centre of the universe as it orbits the sun. That my pencil's not solid, since its subatomic particles are constantly on the move. Justine always had snakes in her hair: I simply couldn't see them. All was there, every bit of past, present, and future, but I was only getting it in increments. If that means we can't take too much reality, *yeah!* That's why we invent stories: the package approach to finding out what's going on. It's terrifying. We shouldn't have to live in such suspense, for crying out loud!

From my window I looked up at the blackness where no stars shone. Malitia had darkened the sky. I looked over the roofs at the domes and towers, and became afraid. In the building opposite a woman stood at her window. Noticing me, she turned away. A breeze came up, carrying with it the fumes of diesel exhaust. In the distance I could hear voices arguing.

I went to bed. During the night I woke to hopeless cries and watched from my window a blood-drenched man stagger unheeded along the street. In the morning I couldn't determine if this was a dream.

32

"I have been expecting you," she said.

She had the most beautiful, irresistible neck I had ever seen: glossy mahogany. I wanted to reach out and stroke it. She smiled. Her teeth were uneven but nonetheless charming. "You are Robert Poley, no?"

Her eyes. Oh my God, her eyes. Deep burgundy.

"Yes," I said.

She held out her hand. "I am Oumou Sangaré."

I wiped the sweat from my hand and shook hers. As I expected, it was cool, firm, silky.

"Come in."

I went into the house that had once been rented by International Ventures, where Christo Mercer had written his fantasy of Salma and Sarra, the house he'd left on the day he went out to meet his death. This was a house of marble floors and Persian carpets. Ornate arches separated rooms, and curtains hung where doors should've been. Kelims decorated the walls. The room she led me to had modern furniture: metal and leather, uncomfortable. The chairs were arranged round a glass coffee table; on a stainless-steel trolley against the wall stood a television set and a video player.

We sat down. I looked at her, and she returned the gaze.

"Who told you to expect me?" I asked.

She shrugged. Not a single crease or blemish visible on her neck.

"I was told."

"By Kleinsmidt?"

"I have nothing to do with them anymore."

"Who, then?"

"I can't say."

I took a flyer: "John Campbell?"

She smiled. "What would you like to know, Mr. Poley?"

Again the teeth, the eyes. The elegance of her neck.

"I would like to know what happened," I replied.

"There is much that happened," she said. "There were sad words, anger, premonitions; there was revenge, an old man's madness; there was treachery, deaths, and lives that went on. There was love, too. And grief."

"Perhaps you should start with the sad words."

Yes, she said, the sad words, unhappy ones that should never have been spoken: words of parting between Christo Mercer and Ibn el-Tamaru.

When Valdes—her nickname for Christo—arrived at Malitia, Ibn el-Tamaru was already there. He had been waiting for two days. He was sickly, coughing blood, his face sucked tightly to his skull, his eyes gone rheumy, crinkled skin hanging from his arms like muslin sleeves. In the slackness of his jaw, in his inward stare, was a profound distraction. He was accompanied by Salma and six bodyguards.

"She has come to see me die," he said to Oumou Sangaré.

"Finally," said Salma.

"You should both have stayed in Djano," Oumou Sangaré replied. "I could've persuaded Valdes to travel."

Ibn el-Tamaru haunted the house. He seemed to inhabit all the rooms simultaneously. He walked on feet so quiet that no one heard his approach or departure. He would appear and disappear, materialize and fade away. Silently he ghosted the house toying with ornaments, running the palm of his hand over the weave of the kelims, sliding the daggers displayed upon the walls in and out of their ornate sheaths. Unsettled, Oumou Sangaré couldn't tell him to visit the cafés or the markets, so the house might recompose itself. She noticed flecks of blood on the tiles. In the night she would wake to hear his coughing faintly below, then suddenly bark in the next room. He never slept.

While they waited through the two long days before Valdes arrived, Oumou Sangaré and Salma watched videos.

"Are you really waiting to see him die?" she asked.

"Yes," said Salma.

"Have you no compassion?"

"No," said Salma.

The screen showed two young men in a room. One was lying on a bed, the other sat on a chair. Then a tall man in a suit entered and began interrogating them, a gun in hand. He ate some of the food that was on a table in front of the sitting man. Abruptly he shot the man lying on the bed, the other gagged with fear as the tall man swung the gun and shot him in the shoulder. A second man, in a darker suit, searched through the cupboard at the back of the room, where eventually he found a briefcase. He opened it and looked inside. He also had a gun, and with his partner started shooting the young man in the chair.

"He's already dead," said Salma. "It's just his body that has to be killed."

Oumou Sangaré waited all afternoon for Valdes' plane to arrive. She watched him disembark. And although he glanced at her waiting beside the fence, didn't wave. He walked to the customs shed, where she knew the officials would let him through without stamping his passport. Suddenly he was in front of her, and they embraced.

"He is waiting for you," she said. "As restless as a fox."

Valdes nodded. "What's he want?"

"He hasn't said. He's brought his crippled daughter. She says she's come to see him die."

"She always says that," said Valdes.

What Ibn el-Tamaru wanted was guns. They stood on the roof in the cooling light, he and Valdes and Oumou Sangaré, and he said he wanted guns, and didn't mind what sort. AKs would be best, but otherwise M16s or R1s, even Uzis, would do. Valdes saw the four girls lying bleeding on the sand. Why did you do it, he wanted to ask, though he could have predicted the answer: "My customs are as peremptory as wrathful planets, death, or destiny." He faced west where the sun had gone.

"Who're they for?" he asked.

Oumou Sangaré translated.

"For me," Ibn el-Tamaru replied.

His words came to Valdes through Oumou Sangaré's uneven teeth.

"Why, after all these years?" asked Valdes.

"To stop the imperialists," the warlord replied. "They take

our oil, they mine our wealth. They come with their loans and their aid packages and their machines and promises of technology, and soon we are trapped in debt. You have seen the beggars. You have seen the women and children scratching in the dirt for gold. Do you know who pays them for their scratchings? The politicians in smart cars. And where do the smart cars come from? The Americans. But what the politicians don't understand is that one day the imperialists will send their planes to bomb our cities. The day we cannot pay our debt, their soldiers will come to kill us and take whatever we have left."

"Bullshit," said Valdes. "Better to say it is Allah's will."

He shook his big head. He was thinking of Oumou Sangaré's breasts, wanting to lay his head on them and listen to her heart. "No," he said.

"No?"

Ibn el-Tamaru coughed. He spoke again, once the spasms subsided, but his voice at first was a harsh whisper.

"I do not understand," he said. "You are my friend. You are not like the others—the French, the Italians, the Polish, the Russians, the Czechs. They all play two-faced games. But you understand our cause. You have not denied me before."

"Before it wasn't for you," said Valdes.

"Sell them to him," Salma called out behind them. No one had noticed her as she climbed slowly, dragging her leg, up the stairs to the roof. "It is better for a friend to take his money than some foreigner."

"See?" said Ibn el-Tamaru. "My daughter understands."

"She says she has come to see you die," said Oumou Sangaré. "Those aren't the words of a daughter."

"I am not his daughter," Salma said quietly.

"Take what you want," said Valdes. "Only let me sleep."

That night Christo Mercer dreamt he and Wilma were sailing

on a yacht. They passed an island where the prisoners were digging lime, and strange men wrapped in blankets stood along the shore. Naked lepers washed in the rock pools. The island disappeared. Wilma put her hand into the water and whipped it back, screaming that the ocean was charged with electricity. Christo Mercer went over the side to show she was wrong. He lay in the sea reading a book. A giant cuttlefish—its eyes huge and bulging, its mouth grinning, its tentacles streaming behind it—rose up towards him through the blue. He could see it clearly. He knew he could be eaten whole.

Oumou Sangaré woke him as he thrashed amidst the sheets that were tentacles encircling his life.

"You shouldn't have let him take the guns," she said.

"It doesn't matter," Valdes replied.

In the morning, Ibn el-Tamaru and his men were gone. Valdes spent the day writing. Salma worked a tapestry of plastic beads she'd bought in the market. Now it was Oumou Sangaré who drifted about the house. She cleaned the rusty specks of Ibn el-Tamaru's blood from the tiles. She returned the ornaments to their places. When she took coffee to Valdes, he didn't even look up from his laptop. She watched CNN until, three days later, she saw Ibn el-Tamaru on the news. She recorded the clip, made Valdes watch it, and he went screaming in rage up to Salma's room.

Salma heard him shouting. She heard Oumou Sangaré calling after him. She leant against the table with the blood quickening through her. The door slammed back against the wall and Valdes, red-faced, hurled himself into the room.

"What is he doing?" he shouted.

He pounded the table and then grabbed her arm, wrenching her so she fell against him; her cheek flattened on the sweatiness of the chest hairs bunching from his shirt. He dragged her towards the door. Oumou Sangaré had her other arm and was trying to pull her up, but she couldn't stand because the pain shrieked in her bones. Oumou Sangaré was saying, "Don't worry, don't worry," as they went down the stairs trailing Salma's legs, with each step the jolts firing into her like bullets. She couldn't talk from the pain. She couldn't see through the whiteness that had fastened over her eyes. They rushed along a passage: Valdes ahead, his hand clamped around Salma's wrist; Oumou Sangaré supporting her as best she could and still gasping, "Don't worry, it's all right, don't worry."

Salma wanted to scream at them to stop, but she could barely breathe. They entered the room decorated with leather and steel, and Valdes released her. He pointed at the television set, to a blurred picture of men and bodies flickering on the screen, and kept shouting in his frightening, incomprehensible language, gesticulating at the picture with the remote control.

"It's your father," Oumou Sangaré said. "It's Ibn el-Tamaru on the news."

The picture began to move: the men walking among the bodies, flames striking up from the thatch of the mud huts. Some women stood weeping, holding babies, their children clutching at them. Another woman was bent wailing over a body, her mouth open in a howl that couldn't be heard.

The camera moved to Ibn el-Tamaru in his black robes. He was holding a gun, his chèche undone to expose his face.

Then the picture changed to a woman in a bed, surrounded by six pink babies. A man, crouched alongside, was holding her hand. They smiled at the camera.

Valdes pointed the remote control at the screen and it went blue. "What is he doing?" he shouted. "What is he doing?"

He kicked the furniture, hammered his fist against the wall, he reran the tape so that the old warlord, gaunt ibis, walked again among the dead. "Why?" he yelled. "What have they done?"

"It's his way," Salma gasped.

"For twenty-five years he hasn't done this. That's what he told me."

"It will go on until he is killed."

"No!" howled Valdes, knocking a vase from a side table, spilling flowers and water. It shattered on the marble floor. "No," he said. "He cannot."

He rushed from the room.

Oumou Sangaré said to Salma in their language: "There are nine dead. He says he will attack all those who accept money from the West."

Oumou Sangaré let the tape run on. She and Salma watched the woman and the man and the babies.

The voice-over said, "In Little Rock today there was much rejoicing in the Macaskill family when Sharon gave birth to sextuplets. Mother and Judy, Michael, Ronni, Margaret, Joan, and Oscar are all doing fine."

A doctor in a white coat bent over to kiss the crying-laughing Sharon; he shook the man's hand. A nurse stepped in front of the doctor to hand a bunch of flowers to Sharon. They all waved at the camera.

"What do we do now?" asked Oumou Sangaré.

"Wait," said Salma.

In the coming days there was nothing more on CNN. Salma stayed in her room stringing the beads of her tapestry. Valdes wrote. Oumou Sangaré watched television. In the desert a man on a camel was riding towards them with news of the death of Ibn el-Tamaru. He took two days to reach Malitia, and in that time he stopped only to cook his food. He was one of the warlord's cohort, a Tuareg who understood the nature of blood. He rode his camel right to the door of Valdes' house and gave to Oumou Sangaré a package wrapped in plastic bags. Before she could ask anything he rode away.

Oumou Sangaré opened the package alone. Inside were the faded black outfit Ibn el-Tamaru usually wore, and another videotape cassette. She held up the clothes: stained with blood and gritty and shredded where the bullets had torn through them. They stank. She dropped them with a cry.

Although Oumou Sangaré did not want to see the tape, Salma and Valdes did. It showed Ibn el-Tamaru winding the long length of his chèche over his face and head until only his eyes were visible. His men on their camels brandished weapons, their stern eyes glaring from the swathes of their turbans. Next the group thundered across the desert with dust rising in a column behind them to attack an army patrol of five or six men. The fight didn't last long. Ibn el-Tamaru was the only raider to die. All the soldiers were killed.

Valdes said, "Are you happy now?"

"Yes," Salma replied.

"That is all I can tell you," said Oumou Sangaré.

"And where is she now?" I asked.

"Salma? She went back to Djano. Do you want to visit her?"

33

It took three days of hell to drive—in a Toyota Land Cruiser— to Djano. The air conditioner was broken; the air scorched through the windows like dragon's breath. At first we were on a road with other travellers: small caravans of camels, men herding livestock, but also trucks, 4x4s, tourists, soldiers. Beside the road were burnt-out wrecks, the debris of metal and rubber and plastic. On either side stretched a gravel plain. At the horizon the sky pressed down like tin onto the sharp ground. Not even my sunglasses could haze such starkness.

Some time in the afternoon we turned onto a track running

between yellow dunes, through palm groves towards blue distant mountains. We passed mud towns, villages, wadis, Roman ruins. The mountains came nearer, turned to red towers of granite. We went down among sculpted rocks into a long canyon. Flocks of birds flew up before us like smoke. How Martha Gellhorn would've revelled in this. All I could do was imagine my body reduced to the leathered bones we passed: a white man weathered black, now buried in the sand, now exposed again. There were no other travellers in these reaches.

At dusk we stopped near the end of the canyon. The driver put up tents, made a fire, began cooking. Oumou Sangaré and I drank whisky.

"This is a far place, no, Mr. Poley?" she said.

I nodded. My tongue didn't want to talk: it wanted to lie in the pool of liquor I held in my mouth.

"Many times we've stopped here because Valdes didn't like the open desert. He preferred to be between the cliffs. He said the space invaded him and created deserts in his head."

"Did you and Valdes grieve at the death of Ibn el-Tamaru?" I asked with more sarcasm than I meant.

"What is grief, Mr. Poley?" She turned those eyes on me. "Is it tears? Or sadness? Is it anger? You are a writer; you should know about such things."

I mumbled an apology.

"You know we were lovers, Mr. Poley? This was no secret. It wasn't always like that. To begin with I was his translator. I travelled wherever he went, into the mountains, into the desert, to places like Djano. But there are some things we cannot escape: love is one of these things. So the inevitable happened. I am not sorry it happened, and I don't think Valdes was either. He was like that with people: you were either close to him or you were nothing in his life. It was because of this that every time he was here we would go to Djano to see his friend, Ibn el-Tamaru. Not always to do business, most times just to talk.

"As you can see, it is not an easy journey. It takes three days. Two nights you have to sleep in the desert, which is a very cold place. Later, when you wake up and your bones are aching, you will wonder if this journey is as important as you thought. You will want to be back in Malitia, where the nights are warm. For someone to go to Djano just for conversation is madness, do you not think so? Well, Valdes had that madness for Ibn el-Tamaru."

She was silent. But when she spoke again her voice seemed to come from a long way off.

"Valdes was never angry; he was always kind. When he went away sometimes I couldn't breathe with longing. When he came back I couldn't see through the tears.

"So, Mr. Poley, for me it was a heartache. Sometimes I pretended he would leave his wife and take me to South Africa. I tried to imagine that. This city of Pretoria. This country of trees and grass and purple blossoms. I have some of that. He brought me purple flowers from the . . . the . . ."

"Jacaranda."

"*Oui*, the jacaranda. But I knew he wouldn't do that. I never spoke of it; what was the use? The way he loved me was not the way he loved his wife. Or his children. It is sad what life does, no?

"Ah, but what do these things matter to you, Mr. Poley? You are not interested in my heart. You want to know did Valdes grieve!

"Let me tell you this, I felt there was something the matter even before he came to Malitia. On the phone he was strange. When I ask him what is the trouble he says he is tired, there is so much work to do, there are problems with the government, maybe the business is finished. Never had he talked like that before. So I knew there were things wrong.

"Valdes was not a happy man, but he was not a sad man either. He was a serious man. He did not see life as a game. To him life was—how do you say it?—character. The way people behaved told him their values. Those that made jokes were worthless. Those that realized how their lives were going, like Ibn el-Tamaru, those were the people Valdes sought. He believed in fate. You have another word for it: destiny. It is a better word, it gives to us some control of the lives we live.

"Valdes knew what was happening in his destiny. Before he came here, he knew that. And I knew it. The arrival of Ibn el-Tamaru and Salma told me that things were not normal. Ibn el-Tamaru was so nervous. I have never seen him like that, except when his wife died.

"That was a strange thing, Mr. Poley. For years they did not speak to one another. They did not even see one another. Then the next we hear she has eaten glass and died. And Ibn el-Tamaru became a shattered man. He was not the same after her death. He and Valdes didn't talk so much after that: of course they still met, they played chess, but they seemed to prefer silence to words. Myself, I do not think the old man ever stopped grieving for his wife, no matter what had gone bad between them.

"It was then this funny business started with Salma. Suddenly she was always with him. He blamed her for Sarra's death yet would go nowhere without her. Every time I saw her she said she was there only to watch him die. I don't like that one, Mr. Poley; she gives me problems.

"Especially that last time. She knew what he was going to do and she wanted him to do it. She sat in her room making that tapestry, waiting for him to kill himself. I don't care what it was he did to her. That was history. Ever since, he had looked after her like a daughter. But she couldn't forgive him. Not for one moment, never. Always she hated him.

"So now you can see how uncomfortable it was. This upset man. This nasty woman. Then comes Valdes. And he, too, is strange. I feel he has gone away from me. He lets Ibn el-Tamaru have guns even when he knows what is going on. Suddenly it is as if he doesn't care anymore. He spends all the time writing. At night we make love but without meaning. It is just two bodies rubbing together. *Phsst*. Over. Go to sleep.

"He has nightmares; I wake him. He goes back to sleep and has more nightmares. Myself, I do not have dreams, Mr. Poley. But Valdes has them from the moment he shuts his eyes. He talks, he shouts, he screams, he jerks sometimes about the bed so badly he fell off. This was frightening.

"Then we get the clothes and the videotape. Salma doesn't say anything. She doesn't claim gladness or relief or pleasure, nothing. She just packs up and goes back to Djano.

"Valdes doesn't say anything, either. One day I find him crying. Another day I find him tearing his book into shreds. He is angry. The vein in his neck is standing out like a water pipe. His face is so flushed I fear for his heart. He has ripped the covers off the book. He is tearing each page into long strips, one page at a time. That is the book he took with him everywhere. *Tamburlaine*. Every night it used to lie on the table beside the bed. Whenever we went away it went with us. 'What are you doing?' I scream at him. 'It is finished, Oumou,' he shouts; 'it is all over.' I didn't know what he was talking about.

"After that he doesn't do any more writing. He starts going out to the cafés. He comes back drunk. I plead with him not to do this, but he tells me it is business, that there are men he has to meet. Never before has he done business this way. Never before have I seen him drunk. There was nothing I could do, Mr. Poley. When they came to tell me he was killed, it was almost a relief. Do you understand that, almost a relief."

34

In the night, when it was as cold as Justine's heart, I lay awake listening to the earth groan. It cracked. It whispered. It sighed. I put my head beneath the pillow but still could hear scorpions scuttling across the sand. Some places should never be visited because they contain too much hostility, too many insects. This was a prime example. In the morning we were hunted by flies.

We drove into the desert, through reaches unbroken by either rocks or distant mountains.

"It is this part that made Valdes uneasy," Oumou Sangaré said.

We drove and the desert didn't change. The driver played the tapes of Youssou N'Dour that Christo Mercer must have listened to.

In the afternoon, out of nowhere, came the palm trees of an oasis: dwellings and a shop that sold petrol and Cokes.

"Robert," Oumou Sangaré said while we sipped our Cokes and waited for the petrol to be pumped, "you would have liked Valdes."

I was no longer Mr. Poley. Somewhere we had crossed a line in the sand and I had changed. I was now Hrubirt. I could have listened to her say that name a thousand times.

Robert. Hrubirt.

As we had the first day, we went on until sunset. Yet where we stopped was nowhere: a featureless halt in an empty plain. It must have shifted the fear of immensity like cold blood across Christo Mercer's brain. Out there you were exposed to the universe.

That night Oumou said to me: "Robert, there is something I want to do."

She paused.

We were sitting about the fire, eating. We did not look at one another. I knew what she was going to say.

"I want to make love."

I didn't respond except to close my eyes, but she could not have seen that in the dark.

"You are embarrassed?" she asked.

I thought of AIDS. I had no condoms. If you have sex with her you'll die, I thought.

"Now you are making me embarrassed," she said.

I chose to risk death.

35

Post coitum omne animal triste.

36

Salma: One day, long after Sarra died, Ibn el-Tamaru came to see me here in this room, where we did the tapestries. He was already like a skeleton. After climbing the stairs he was breathing with difficulty. Wheezing.

He wanted to say something but he couldn't, he had to gasp for air.

I kept repeating at him in my head: you are guilty, you are guilty, you are guilty. I couldn't stop because I feared what was underneath. I was afraid of my own weakness. I was afraid I might forgive him. But I couldn't. He was guilty. I had to accuse him. What he was and what he'd become couldn't be separated.

He had killed them: Farida, Dirie, Gali. When he attacked Djano my mother and father were killed by his bandits.

He stood before me. If I forgave I would not be freed. I would still have the pain. I would not be healed. I would still be ashamed that I had been allowed to live. It would be too easy to forgive him, too easy.

So my choice was to accuse him. To judge him. Like the ibis I had to judge him. I had to. For those who were dead. But not only for them, also for those who had chosen to forget.

Once if a person had leprosy he had to warn people of his disease. He had to ring a bell as he went. I was Ibn el-Tamaru's bell. I reminded him of what he was.

I do not think there can be any forgiving and there should be no forgetting. Ibn el-Tamaru was a killer and he will always be that and so forever he will be unforgiven. For me, though, it is no longer a matter of not forgetting what he did, it is that I no longer need to remember. I have my graves to tend. I have my memories. I have my life. I still have the pain but it is now the pain of an old wound that didn't kill me. I survived. It reminds me that I survived.

Of course I think often of Sarra, but it is the same with her memory: I don't ache for her anymore. The anger of grief is gone. Instead I smile whenever I think I see her at the corner of my eye. Time has passed. I have come to accept this story of my life.

Once, many years ago, Sarra taught me to read and write. She did this with a story about a man called Ghanim the Distraught, the Thrall o' Love. In those days I thought it was just a story of an unlucky man who has to suffer until suddenly his life entered years of good fortune. Now I know she wanted to show me how destiny deals with us.

So, I look out and see that everywhere Djano is in decay, of no interest to anyone but these young tourists in their trucks.

Many people have left. The houses are crumbling. The wells are drying up. The water is full of guinea worm. In the cafés there are those who want back the days of Ibn el-Tamaru and even some who want back the days of the French.

I don't want either. I want now. I want this heat and the colour on the dunes when the sun goes down, and I want even the ruins here in the town. I want to live here until I die. I want to be buried here.

One day Djano will again be part of the dunes. No one will be able to see our lives here. Maybe then some person will come to dig in the ruins and maybe she will find between my bent bones a bullet. Maybe she will find the grave where my mother and father are buried with all those others. Maybe she will find the graves of my friends with more bullets among their bones. Or Sarra's grave with glass in her skeleton. Maybe then this person will wonder how we lived here.

(Personal interview [translated by Oumou Sangaré]: Djano; 9 November 1995)

37

History is not one of my subjects. I do not hear stones speak. They speak to Justine, they have volumes to say to her, but to me they are mute, they are stones. A ruin is a ruin.

Sure, when we did Justine's European Massacre tour I could wonder at those fields of small white crosses in northern France, but I couldn't imagine the bodies behind them. In Dachau I could see a monument but couldn't feel the suffering. Justine would be weeping at my side; I would be numb with the cold. At Lidice I could watch Nazi film footage of Germans machine-gunning the village men, loading the women into cattle trucks, razing the village, but I had to keep telling myself that in 1942 it really happened. It seemed so much like a war video to me.

"Jesus, Robert, don't you have any compassion?" is the charge Justine brings against me.

When the Wall came down—yet another collection of stones—Justine wanted a piece, of course.

"It's bricks and mortar," I said.

"It's history," she responded.

How she did it I don't know, but she got her fragment of history: a 10 cm long by 5 cm broad piece of cement that could have come from anywhere. That it came with a certificate of authenticity was one of the best marketing campaigns I've seen in years. It must have raised millions. That ornament (such is what history becomes) was one of the few artifacts that escaped her wrath on the night of the rampant Medusa. Presumably it still resides in its Perspex casing on her mantelpiece.

The point is that, for the most part, history leaves me . . . vacant. I can't imagine it.

Even when I'm told, "Here, Mr. Poley, here on this spot is where I was shot," I look down at the sand and see footprints and hoofprints and donkey dung. I do not see blood.

"Your trouble, Robert, is that the only real stuff going on in your head, if you call those juvenile fantasies you write real, is fiction. You can't see the world we live in." This was Justine's diagnosis on one recent occasion (Christmas Day, actually) when I was trying to get some sense out of her.

So I could stand with Salma and Oumou outside Djano with the sun only just up and the old town still washed with its redness as it had been on that day in 1970 when, to put it in the euphemistic terms of historiography, the old warlord freed it from the last vestiges of French colonialism, and I could think: what am I doing here?

And I could remind myself: you are here to imagine an atrocity in order to keep it from being forgotten. You are here to imagine the deaths of the three girls and the wounding of Salma. You are here to imagine how at another city, the city of Damascus, four virgins were speared to death and their bodies pinioned to the city's wall. You are here to imagine why Christo Mercer chose this as his metaphor. But I couldn't.

I looked at the sand. I picked it up and let it trickle through my fingers, the sand that Salma had collapsed on, that others had died on, and it was just sand.

"It's not failure of the imagination, my dear Robert; it's that there comes a point where, thank God, we remain strangers to one another" was Professor Khafulo's assessment of the human condition (21 October 1995). "How you experience life is not the way I do."

And who am I to argue with him!

I have stood on the sand where Christo Mercer stood while he imagined the gunmen shooting his four teenagers. I have walked the streets of Malitia. I have eaten lunch in the café where he had his last meal. I have even slept with his lover. But who is Christo Mercer? And why was he stabbed?

38

On the morning of his death, Christo Mercer left Oumou Sangaré sleeping and went out alone. He was dressed in jeans and a T-shirt. Over his shoulders was a light jacket worn in the European manner of a summer evening, with the sleeves dangling empty. He had on soft leather shoes. He was unarmed. His head hurt and his mouth tasted of onions.

It was late in the morning, close to midday, because Christo Mercer had spent most of the previous night watching Vietnam videos: *The Deer Hunter, Platoon, Full Metal Jacket*.

After the first two, Oumou Sangaré said, "That's enough, Valdes," to which he responded by putting on *Full Metal Jacket*.

He was drinking whisky, had finished a bottle and started a second. When the video ended, he was too drunk to walk, and Oumou Sangaré had to drag him upstairs to bed.

When he left her in the morning, she was only pretending sleep: she heard him shower, she heard him dress, she heard him close the street door. Then she turned onto her back and opened her eyes. She stared up at the ceiling and thought: what's happening to him?

Eight hours later, the police came to tell her. She remembered it was dark, that she had to switch the lights on. They told her the news in the room with the leather furniture. She was too shocked to cry. She felt relieved. Her headache stopped but its shadow pain lingered at her temples.

"Where is he?" she asked.

They took her to the morgue.

For those eight hours Oumou Sangaré had occupied herself with domestic chores. After lunch she told the servants they need not come in again that day. In the early afternoon, she slept for an hour on the back verandah until the heat woke her; she was wet with perspiration. Again she thought: what's happening to him? But then she put the thought from her mind, and showered and changed to go shopping for groceries. The market distracted her for a while from the pain building behind her eyes. Later she sorted through a folder of accounts and mended a broken lamp. Then, towards sunset, a breeze came up and she opened the house to the air and stood in the draught with her arms out like a landing ibis. The pain tightened in her head. She had no appetite but ate some fruit for supper. The breeze faltered and the rooms stopped whispering. Oumou Sangaré lay in the dark with an ice pack clamped to her forehead. As she was doing when the policeman told her Christo Mercer was dead.

When he left Oumou Sangaré late on the morning of the day he was to die, Christo Mercer went to the International Café. He'd frequented the place for a few hours every day since the death of Ibn el-Tamaru, or, more precisely, since he'd torn up his copy of Marlowe's *Tamburlaine*. He would sit at the same table against the wall with the snowy heights of Mont Blanc towering over him. The walls of the International Café honoured European landmarks: the Arc de Triomphe, Trafalgar Square, Cologne cathedral, the Bridge of Sighs. Sometimes Christo Mercer would read listlessly in old copies of the *International Herald Tribune* or *Time* magazine, but mostly he would sit staring at the door, waiting. He would order first a coffee and then a whisky. A coffee and then a whisky. He was always drunk when he left.

He was "a possessed man," according to François, the café's proprietor. He was a "gentleman," according to Abdul, the waiter.

"But so what?" added François. "We've had possessed men coming here since I opened in 1956."

"He left good gratuities," said Abdul.

On the last day of Christo Mercer's life, the International Café was as busy as ever. In the morning, before he got there, Abdul had served gâteaux and cream cappuccinos to the wives of ambassadors and financiers and construction engineers. At lunch he served medallions of veal and zucchini to their husbands.

It was lunchtime when Christo Mercer came in with three men and sat down at his usual table beneath the mountain.

"His face was hopeful," said François. "He didn't look like a man who was about to die."

They ordered champagne. They wanted Moët but François had only Veuve Clicquot.

"They were lucky," said François. "In Malitia there is no call to drink champagne."

Abdul poured the wine. The men clinked glasses.

François went through his menu for the day. He recommended the veal. Christo Mercer insisted on lobster. The short man in the suit who sat beside him ordered sole, the other two—to François they were land surveyors—had the medallions of veal.

"They were English," said François. "They were all Englishmen."

Once they'd finished eating they drank cold white wine all through the afternoon. At times they were the only patrons, and Abdul dozed in the heat while their conversation droned on like flies over a carcass. Once the short man woke him by dripping water from the ice bucket onto his eyelids, and the group laughed at Abdul's startled curse. They teased him and Abdul grinned sheepishly at their jokes. They wanted coffee: double espressos.

"They were customers," said Abdul. "I didn't mind their jokes."

The men settled back to their conversation. They weren't arguing, merely discussing, and there was no anger in their voices. Mostly they talked quietly, Christo Mercer having as much to say as any of them. Sometimes they fell silent for long moments.

In the late afternoon, when François returned from his siesta, the café started filling up again, this time with aid workers and NGO staff and French-language teachers. They were young and noisy and drank milky-coloured aperitifs. Abdul was revived by their enthusiasm and the cool breeze that came in from the street to help the ceiling fans that had hardly stirred the air during the hot hours. Christo Mercer and his companions ordered aperitifs. Their conversation had stopped.

"They were looking tired," said François. "They looked like men who had been on a journey."

"They left good gratuities," said Abdul. "The short one paid. American Express card."

The men stood and Christo Mercer shook hands with each one of them. They all met his eyes and one of the "surveyors" said something which caused Christo Mercer to shrug. The "surveyor" looked at the short man and both made gestures of resignation. The men threaded their way through the tables and went outside, parting without lingering; the short man reached up and patted Christo Mercer on the back. For a brief moment Christo Mercer watched them walk away, then he turned in the opposite direction. The sun had set but it was not yet dark.

An hour later Christo Mercer was killed less than a hundred metres from where François and Abdul were welcoming their first evening patrons. He was attacked by two men, who stabbed him fifteen times.

39

I do not know what the truth is about Christo Mercer's death. All I have are the facts and the theories.

"Look at the facts, Robert. The facts are that we're not compatible anymore. I don't want to eat another soggy pizza."

Or.

"I don't care what theories you have about menopause and hot flushes, Robert. I know what I feel. Theories don't count."

In a way Justine is right, theories don't count. We have the facts: Christo Mercer is dead. Justine is in love with a woman. But all the same we—or I—want to know why. So we—or I—postulate (à la Professor Khafulo) various theories.

To start with, there's the question of homosexuality.

If Justine—that former connoisseur of lifesavers' tight buns—could suddenly switch her attention to Madonna-cone boobs, why couldn't Christo Mercer have a craving to grab another man's balls? To the inquest magistrate this was clearly what was going on. The two young men found guilty of the killing were known rent-boys. It was presumed that somewhere in his transactions with them something went horribly wrong, as the saying goes. All one can really argue is that this theory accounts for the last hour before his death.

But.

Mary Fitzgerald: "Was Christo a closet? No. Absolutely not. Christo hated homosexuals. He thought they were sick, perverted people" (Telephone interview; 20 December 1995).

Martin Eloff: "I am gay, Mr. Poley. In order to keep our friendship I kept this side of my life hidden from Christo. One of the most wounding things about him was his vehemence against homosexuality. Certainly, if he'd found out about me, he would've refused to have anything more to do with me. I know it is fashionable to say that those who are virulently homophobic are repressing hidden proclivities, but the mind boggles at the thought of Christo buying sex from some back-street trader. No, personally, I think it's just an easy way out for the Malitia authorities" (Telephone interview; 20 December 1995).

Oumou Sangaré: "It's nonsense, Robert. Probably the boys didn't even kill Valdes. They were, how do you say it, stooged!" (Personal interview: Malitia; 14 November 1995).

Which brings me to the highly unlikely Theory Number Two: suicide by attack. This, of course, is Martin Eloff's explanation, but how much weight does one really give in these matters to the publicity manager of a five-star hotel? Certainly I can concede that Christo Mercer was obsessed—to the point of weirdness—with the death of the four virgins in Marlowe's *Tamburlaine the Great*. He was, probably, depressed. Anxiety attacks tortured his nights. He was having horrendous dreams —admittedly nothing new to him, but a factor nonetheless. He was also probably distraught at the death of Ibn el-Tamaru. But is all this enough to make him provoke two hapless young thugs into stabbing him fifteen times? Did he really want a copycat death in the Ibn el-Tamaru tradition? No, Mr. Eloff, I doubt it. Even if he went to the aid of a tourist being mugged, even if in the course of being mugged himself he turned macho, I can't see two hoodlums putting their knives in and out of him for a total of fifteen times. Fifteen times seems to me like assassination.

And assassination is the theory of the three (to coin a word) conspiratorialists: P. J. P. Mostert (Mossad), Mary Fitzgerald (South African hit squad), Oumou Sangaré (either of the above or else dealers from another country who were protecting their territory). As this is the theory with all the unanswered and unanswerable questions, it also comes closest to my pulp-fiction heart; it embodies "the weaving of the desired tapestry," to borrow a phrase.

So, who were those mysterious men who bought Christo Mercer his last lunch?

Was NS—Nicholas Skeres—among them?

"I do not know this man, Hrubirt. Valdes never spoke of such a man," says Oumou Sangaré.

"Did he mention an Englishman?" I persist.

"Maybe. Perhaps. There are lots of Englishmen. The world is full of Englishmen selling guns."

True enough. What, however, took them a whole afternoon to discuss? And where was Christo Mercer during the unaccountable hour?

Ah, but this hints at dark and devious doings.

"Indeed, my dear Robert, it does," confirms my literary adviser, "and perhaps at this point you should consider the Elizabethans more closely. After all this is the sort of shadow world so many of them walked in, particularly our friend Marlowe. So may I refer you to Charles Nicholl's excellent if academically problematic thriller *The Reckoning* (London: Jonathan Cape, 1992).

"Nevertheless, as I've told you before, Nicholl's rather good on Marlowe's death. But there's much more I can add. Why don't we meet for a drink and I'll elaborate? It's so difficult discussing matters over the phone. Also, I want to hear all about your trip."

Back off, Professor. I'm trying to do some serious research here.

On page 327 Nicholl argues that Marlowe (read Mercer) "did not die by mischance, and he was not killed in self-defence. He had become an impediment to the political ambitions of the Earl of Essex [or any major apartheid advocate now trying to cover his tracks]. His lackeys had tried to frame him; to get him imprisoned and tortured; to use him as their 'instrument' against Ralegh [akin to someone like P. W. Botha]. They had tried all this and failed. He had proved elusive, a danger. . . . His mouth—if it could not be made to say what they wanted it to say—must be 'stopped'. . . . I do not think the purpose of the meeting was murder. . . . Rather, Marlowe's death was a decision. It was a point the day reached, by a process of dwindling options. . . . The killing happens in the hermetic confines of the secret world: a dirty trick, a rogue event, a tragic blunder."

Ah ha! A dirty trick. A rogue event. A tragic blunder.

Beads for an ibis tapestry.

40

Late yesterday afternoon (Sunday, 14 January 1996) I wrote those words, the last of my "little project." Outside in the palm tree the laughing doves were laughing: koo koo kuRUkutu-koo.

Above the city the mountain rose blue through the heat. Pushed under my door was a crazy letter from Justine that I "come over and have a drink and meet Toni." On the answering machine were a spate of messages:

"Robert, I do think you should have the decency to return my calls. After all the time I spent helping you and the effort it took to read some of that ridiculous stuff you insisted I analyze, the very least one expects is some show of courtesy if not gratitude. I must admit I've not encountered such rudeness since 1962 when I tried to walk down Commissioner Street on the pavement. If you can't bring yourself to face me, a letter of apology for your bad manners and thanks for my work would be in order. This, by the way, is Richard."

"Hullo, dear, I've been wondering how you've been getting on. Perhaps when you've got a moment you could give your mother a call. Bye."

"Howzit, Dad, it's Luke. Er . . . [longish pause] agh, nothing really."

Some things are never over.

Today I sat down at Christo Mercer's laptop, booted it up, and opened a file called "dealer.txt." At the top of the screen I typed the title: "Who Markets the Sword," and then began the next airport blockbuster by Robert Poley:

He looked down at her perfect body asleep on the white sheets. She was lying turned away from where he'd been nestling against her: her black hair was spread over the pillow, her breasts were exposed, and he could still feel how her nipples had puckered as he'd explored them with his tongue. Her body was the colour of dark honey. She looked like an Arabian princess.

Christo Mercer grinned at the stir in his groin. He zipped up his Levi's and splashed an Armani fragrance on his cleanly shaven face. A glance at his Tag Heuer told him he had fifteen minutes to walk to the International Café, where no doubt the old warlord, as incorrigible as ever, would already be waiting for him. He slipped the small Beretta into the pocket of his Ralph Lauren linen jacket; there was no point in taking any chances, even though he'd been doing business with the grizzled veteran Ibn el-Tamaru for years. As he went out into Malitia's hot sun he was wondering how many crates of guns he'd be able to sell this time . . .

ALSO BY MIKE NICOL

"Mike Nicol joins the roster . . . of Franz Kafka, Mikhail Bulgakov, Ryszard Kapuściński, and the magical realists of Latin America."   —*The New York Times Book Review*

HORSEMAN

In a village somewhere in Europe, a boy sees his father taken away in chains, and, in his anger and grief, becomes an outlaw. Crossing forests and oceans, mingling with pimps, slavers, and mercenaries, he meets a series of instructors—among them, a hermit who teaches him to survive and a faceless monk who teaches him to kill. In time he calls himself Daupus—a name meaning death—and rides the pale horse foretold in Revelation through a world he will leave in ruins and whose history he will write in blood and fire.

Fiction/0-679-76039-3

THIS DAY AND AGE

With tremendous political daring, South African novelist Mike Nicol offers a luminous parable of his country's past. Bawdy and terrifying, fantastical yet eerily familiar, *This Day and Age* realizes the prophecy told to a newly elected president on the eve of his inauguration. After years of bountiful harmony will come plague and famine, during which a strange man-child with a Bible chained to his wrist and his army of the disenfranchised will gather strength in the most remote reaches of the land.

Fiction/0-679-74200-X